ANCIENT HISTORY

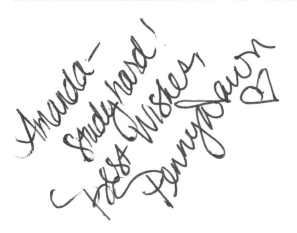

Ancient History

...His hands wandered, feeling every inch of her body, only the thin material of a dancer's garment standing in his way. He caressed his way to the back of the leotard and pulled her a fraction of an inch off the door, his fingers sauntering up her strong back. Did she still purr like a kitten with the slightest caress up her spine?

A throaty sigh against his lips confirmed his musings. Some things—like her last name—had changed over the past five years. But he suspected those primal sounds would remain with her always.

He drew a line along the scoop neck of the leotard with a sudden urge to rip it from her body and feel her naked flesh, to give her the orgasm he'd been dreaming of since he'd left her standing at those intriguing blue windows so many years ago.

Her muscled rear tensed beneath his squeezing fingers, making him even more aware of her strength, her definition, and the fact she wasn't wearing panties. *Oh, Lord.*

Such a beautiful woman. And he had her up against the door, legs in a vertical split and her body encapsulated with his hands like bookends. "Molly."

Her eyes flickered open, steam exuding from her split-second stare, before falling closed again with his next kiss.

The thin garment did little to hide her every curve, but revealing as it was, it stood like a fortress between them, his hands no match for its guard. "I can't find an opening anywhere in this damn thing."

ANCIENT HISTORY

BY

PENNY DAWN

AMBER QUILL PRESS, LLC
http://www.amberquill.com

ANCIENT HISTORY
AN AMBER QUILL PRESS BOOK

This book is a work of fiction. All names, characters,
locations, and incidents are products of the author's imagination,
or have been used fictitiously. Any resemblance to actual persons
living or dead, locales, or events is entirely coincidental.

Amber Quill Press, LLC
http://www.amberquill.com

Layout and Formatting provided by: ElementalAlchemy.com

PUBLISHED IN THE UNITED STATES OF AMERICA

For Mary, who understands my love for Monticello and her great creator.

In memory of the talented and wonderful Nancy Alberts, whose initial commentary drove me to finish the rough draft. She will be missed.

Thanks to my mother Star, whose knowledge of the history of American furniture not only inspired my love affair with antiques, but fed this incredible tale the meat and potatoes it needed to thrive.

I'll never forget those who introduced me to Thomas Jefferson— Henry Schmidt, Lawrence Bock, Judy Bock, and Jill Baker. Ladies and gents, those privileged to have been your students are forever enriched. God bless you, for you are truly inspiring.

My cousin (and cold reader) li'l Kristin inspired Brandywine's straightforward methods.

To the ladies of Tuesday night dance class: it is because of you that Molly became a ballerina.

To the citizens/proprietors of Grayslake: Parker's Landing is a tribute to all of you.

And, as always, thanks to Mary and Angela, who give me from-the-hip reactions, and to my cheerleaders at Seton Hill University, including (but never limited to) Barbara Miller Leslie Guccione, Jacki King, Mark Montgomery, Ana Quinn, Analisa Oviedo, Jillian Slack, and Miles Watson, who attended my erotica reading, although he didn't know he'd like it.

CHAPTER 1

"Something blue from your past calcifies your core center." Molly Rourke's favorite aunt burrowed a wise, brown-eyed stare right through her. "Come in, and tell me all about it."

"I'd rather forget." With a brisk northern Illinois wind blowing at her back, Molly hiked her pink canvas dance bag over her shoulder and entered 171 Park Avenue, a dim, museum-like Victorian. The house was cozy, warm, and comfortable, despite Aunt Star's chillingly accurate intuition regarding Molly's mood.

Star tapped a plump hand against Molly's belly. The signature gold ring on her index finger reflected the dim light. "Hmm." She patted again, this time moving aside the short trench coat. "Are you losing weight again?"

"No."

The copper discs on Star's bracelets chimed against the jade amulet swinging from a leather string around her neck, and the smell of seven-grain bread—homemade, of course—beckoned from the kitchen. "You can't weigh more than one-ten. Come by after ballet class. I'll fatten you up."

"I'm fine."

"You're blue." With fingers flared, Star hitched her generous hips, which sent her orange *dashiki* into a wave. "With a glimpse of patriotism on its wings."

Star sensed Molly had been pondering the stained glass permanently displayed at Chicago's Art Institute, Marc Chagall's

1

America Windows.

"You're a witch, you know that?" Molly tightened her grip on her dance bag.

"You have it, too," Star said. "And you came by your talent much more easily than I."

Five years ago, Molly had happened upon her ability the same way many of her ancestors had—by falling in love with the right man—but Star didn't have to know that. "Drop it, okay? I'm not a prophet, by any stretch of the imagination."

"I wish I could sense the history of a building simply by entering it like you can, Molly."

"I preferred to chalk that up to my experience as an antiquities expert, thank you very much."

"Define it as you will, you—"

"Your premonitions are eerie, Star. And in this particular case, annoying."

"I must be hitting pretty close to the mark then." Star raised an eyebrow.

"Help me out, Chubs." Molly rubbed the cold belly of *Buddha in Headstand*, the terra cotta sculpture occupying a marble pedestal in the parlor. Star respected all gods of all religions—especially fat ones. "Good karma, good karma."

"What you need is a good cleansing and an extra fifteen pounds on your bones. You'll wither away before you reach thirty."

"So I have a few years yet."

"Molly..."

"There's flour on your left breast."

"These things get in the way of everything." Star brushed the white smudge from her bosom and started across the mosaic tiled foyer, stepping over a white-and-grey pile of sheepdog. "Heard from Windy and Joe?"

"I talked to Dad last night. So far no sign of anything paranormal at Blarney Castle."

"Too bad, but come in. You're just in time for Thursday evening toast. A good place to begin." She moved through the archway beneath the stairs to the kitchen. "And I've told you a thousand times, this home's as much yours as it is mine. You don't have to ring the bell."

"The door sticks. I can't open it."

A blender whirred, and Molly's younger cousin Brandywine smiled, sporting lipstick as violet as her leotard and tights. With her hair pulled up in a nosegay of merlot curls, she stood, all curves, before a cast iron farm sink, skirted with red-and-yellow plaid, with a pitcher of green puree in her hand. "What do you say, Mol? We'll convert you sooner or later." She poured the gritty concoction into three tall glasses. *Double shots of Ick.* "Much later." Molly wrinkled her nose at the sight of the wheatgrass. "If ever."

"Have one." Star slinked into a crimson-colored chair and reached for a tumbler of balanced salvation. "To Molly's mysterious blue." Star lifted her glass in salute. "And the path to overcoming it. Let's see what fate has in store for our girl." Star and Brandywine clinked glasses. The younger threw back the shot, but Star sipped it like fine wine.

Molly raised her still-full glass. "To Aunt Star someday purchasing a matching breakfast set and Brandy discovering a new snack." She tossed the contents of her glass into the farm sink. *To Do List: Renege on swearing off ice cream.*

"See you, Star." Brandywine tousled her mother's maroon hair and slipped an arm through Molly's. "And give her a break about the blue, will you? She tells me everything, and there's nothing blue about her."

"I'm not wrong often." Star's eyebrow peaked, and she struck Molly with a demanding stare. "Flush out that blue."

"Sometimes, Aunt Star, you're downright creepy." *Blue.* Chagall had depicted liberty and religious tolerance with blue in his *America Windows*, created in celebration of the United States' bicentennial, but the creation brought no joy to Molly. She'd signed her divorce papers in front of the gorgeous, if not somber, view of freedom on the fifth of May, five years ago today.

She'd come to think of her secret ex-husband—with his sexy Southern drawl and eyes the color of a forest at dawn—as her most fierce passion. And while her ability with old places coincidentally appeared the moment she realized she'd loved him—suggesting they were meant to be—she now knew their union was Fate's biggest mistake.

Brandywine opened the stubborn front door and led her into a calm dusk sweeping its way through the sleepy town of Parker's Landing. The bells of Saint Andrews chimed, announcing the hour of six. They'd be a few minutes late for class. "So what's up, girlfriend?"

"Nothing." Molly quickened her pace across Park Avenue toward Whitney Street.

"The thing about round women: they exaggerate the other end of the spectrum. But Star's right. You do look thinner."

"I weigh the same. One-tenish."

Brandywine fixed her with an intense stare. "Your scale's broken."

Molly sighed. "All right, I didn't eat much today."

"Why not?"

"It was just a busy day."

"And yesterday?"

"Aren't you ever...I don't know...not hungry?"

"No. I can eat six meals a day and seven on Sunday."

"You're lucky you're still thin."

Brandywine grasped her just above the elbow. "I'm not thin, I'm happy."

"And I'm just...preoccupied. It's hard to eat when I can't stop thinking about..." *Him.*

"Thinking about what?"

Molly shook her head. "Nothing." *No one.*

"It would take something pretty phenomenal to draw me away from food."

"Well, you've got that right." The image of Professor Scott Sheridan materialized in Molly's mind, and a strange yearning settled into her skin. *Insane.* He'd swept into her life out of the blue, like a monsoon and left her just as devastated—and in front of blue stained glass. "I thought I'd put this to rest, that's all."

"Put what to rest?"

"Never mind." Why was she yearning for his touch, when all he really deserved was a good smack across his chiseled cheek? And why did she feel as if he were about to appear around the next corner when five years ago, he'd disappeared into Virginia as if she'd drop-kicked him there?

"Promise me you'll eat tonight."

Molly nodded. But the panging in her gut said *no way.* He was close. She could feel it. And who could think of food when she had something as delectable as her gorgeous ex on the tip of her tongue? Another morsel she'd regret in the morning. And just like ice cream, he'd go straight to her hips.

*   *   *

Scott Sheridan double-checked the scrawled address on a coffee-stained napkin. 221 Center Street. He looked up at the narrow storefront, pale pink with ivory gingerbread molding. *Oh, hell.*

He could live with the mad scramble to make the last-minute flight out of Charlottesville, Virginia. He'd dealt with the crazy commuters at O'Hare Airport's taxi stand and the should-be-illegal fare he'd paid for the ride out to this humble 'burg, considering a Metra Train could have delivered him for a few bucks. *Who knew? But this...*

"Amelia's Dance Connection." He read the shingle aloud, as if hearing it would confirm his worst nightmare. According to his online search, this was where Molly lived. No exterior stair led to an apartment, although the second-floor windows suggested living space above. No mailbox. No sign of the brown-eyed beauty anywhere. *Great time to fumble on research, professor, when time is of the essence.*

He glanced up and down Center Street. Like a page out of a history book, hordes of old cars were parked to the west, in front of the Charlie's Pub. A dim light protruded from the bookstore window across the street. Wrought iron lampposts. Benches beneath arbors on cobblestone walks. Intersections marked with forest green obelisks about five feet high, with street names lettered on them in white script.

And the scent of a recently thawed lake wafted on the breeze. If he had more time, he might have cast in a line to unwind before facing her.

With a sharp intake of air, he fingered the size four-and-a-half ring he always kept with him. Today, he'd pinned it into his left trouser pocket. Scrolls of white gold, a hexagonal sapphire, and four diamond baguettes. An antique as precious and irreplaceable as the woman who briefly wore it. And if this were his only lead, Good Lord, he'd follow it. He patted his rear right pocket—where he usually kept a special ten-of-hearts—for courage.

A rotund woman and a large, white-and-grey sheepdog rounded the post at the corner of Whitney and Center, both bounding toward him with reckless abandon. If he believed in predetermined destiny, he might have considered it a sign. Climb the steps or risk being run down—or worse, caught in a conversation with a townie, for whom he simply didn't have time.

He darted up the steps, turned the knob, and entered a comfortable, warm lobby—pink, of course—with rippling hardwood floors the color of molasses. An old church pew served as a bench, and modular wooden cubes on the far side of the room housed shoes and sweaters. Through an interior, leaded glass door standing slightly ajar filtered soft notes of the classical variety.

Curious, Scott peered at the dancers' images, distorted through the glass. *Women. Not girls. Could one of them be—*

He inched the door open. "Good golly, Miss Molly," he whispered.

Amid several other women on the natural maple floors, he spied her, balancing on the ball of her left foot, her shapely right leg propped on the highest *barre*, her left arm arcing over the full, auburn bun in her hair and reaching for the black ballet slipper on her right foot.

He drew in a long, shuddering breath. When had inhalations become such a challenge? Then again, he'd found it hard to breathe every time he'd laid eyes on her.

Clad in a pink leotard, the type that wrapped her thin body seamlessly from ankles to shoulders, she looked good enough to eat. He grinned. He'd have to do that later. "Molly, Molly, Molly."

She faltered from her position this time, pressing her chest to the leg propped on the *barre*, and turned her chocolate eyes in his direction. Upon meeting his gaze, she promptly pinched them shut and shook her head, whispering an expletive through the classical music filling the room.

He looked alternately at her face and at the reflection of her scrumptious rear in the mirror across the studio. *Damn, what a position to find her in.*

A middle-aged woman with a salt-and-pepper ponytail, presumably the Amelia mentioned on the sign outside, pushed a button on her remote control, silencing the music. "May I help you?"

"He's beyond help." Molly straightened, lifted her leg from the *barre*, and pressed her pointed right toe to the curve of her left knee. She shot an icicle glare in his direction. "And he was just leaving."

Well, that solved one mystery. She hated him. Considering she thought he'd left her to study what turned out to be a false boyhood journal of Thomas Jefferson's, could he blame her? He shoved his hands into his pockets, grasping the ring for silent support, and laid the drawl on thick. "You can't spare five minutes for your husband?"

"Oh my, Amin Ra." A younger woman in purple pulled her leg from its post. "Husband?"

"Relax, Brandy." Molly yanked a yellow hand towel from the *barre*, dabbed her glistening forehead, and took a step toward him. "He's not my husband."

"I was once." He watched her jaw clench. "One hell of a time, wasn't it?"

"Sorry for the interruption," his ex-wife said to her classmates, not breaking eye contact with him. "I won't be long." She closed the gap between them, looking flushed, limber, and thinner than he remembered. But sexier than ever.

Curling tendrils of copper hair draped about her temples, and the sprinkling of fine freckles on her nose meant she wasn't wearing make-up. Good, since it was about time she realized she didn't need it. Her full, tawny lips pursed, and when he smiled, she swatted his arm with the towel and physically turned him toward the lobby.

Her fingers on his arm sent a fervent sensation through him. Or maybe it was the faint aroma of lilac emanating from her hair, pulling serene memories from deep within his subconscious. Whatever it was, his mouth went dry and his muscles began to tense with her touch. The tiny lobby faded into a hazy kaleidoscope of stars around her, her face the center of a colorful burst. *Bewitching.*

The resuming music and Molly's closing of the leaded glass door behind her zapped him back to reality. "Molly."

"Are you insane?" She hissed more than spoke. "Do I drop in on your life unexpectedly? Do I drop in at all?"

"No, I—"

"And what a day you've chosen. May fifth." She pushed a stray hair from her temple. "How did you know where to find me?"

"This was your last recorded address."

"Oh."

"You live here?"

"No, I live one block over, on Park. But I rented the apartment upstairs until I followed a deranged history professor on a whirlwind tour that ended…abruptly, shall we say?"

"I'm sorry."

She focused on him again, an emotion somewhere between shock and disbelief registering in her eyes. "You're…what?"

Had he never apologized for their mess of a relationship before? "I'm sorry. There. Five years too late, but double the repentance."

"What do you want?"

"I need to call in a favor."

"I don't owe you a damn thing. Call someone else." She pulled all her weight, albeit not much, up on the ball of one foot and twirled like a statuette in a jewelry box toward the studio. "Perhaps an old girlfriend who actually met your mother."

No one had met his mother in fifteen years, thanks to his father's fist and a shot to the heart with the very revolver intended for her protection, but he couldn't dredge all that up now. Besides, he hadn't met her family either. During their month-long marriage, they'd had

7

more intense meetings on their agenda—most involving hotel mattresses.

"It's about Monticello, Molly."

She stopped in her tracks, her pointed left toe bobbing against the floor, but she did not turn to face him. "Jefferson's Monticello?"

"Do you know another?"

"So, the truth comes out. This is about your job. Always a one-track mind with you."

"It may not be our history, Mol, but it's the history of our country. Monumental."

She sighed, touching a feminine ringlet springing out from her bun. "As usual."

"I have an opportunity to spend a semester on the plantation grounds, revamping and furnishing the Dome Room...the entire second and third floors, as a matter of fact. If all goes well, it'll be open to select tour groups for study this time next year. It's a once in a lifetime chance."

"And they gave it to you. Congratulations. And thanks for taking the pains to let me know about it."

"Well, that's just it, cupcake. Manifest Destiny. I see this as my right, but it isn't mine yet. I know Jefferson better than anyone—"

"Yes, I seem to recall."

"—but Wilkinson at the University of Virginia has an impressive lineup, and I don't have a furniture expert on my team."

Molly met his gaze over her shoulder, and, for a split second, she might have softened. But quickly, her glance turned rock-hard. "In that case, maybe you should've paid more attention to the one you once had."

"I deserve this chance—and the grant that comes with it. I'm a good historian."

"At least you're a good something. You were a lousy husband. My regards to Professor Wilkinson." With that, she yanked the studio door open and scurried to her position on the floor.

He let out a held breath and sank against the wall, watching through the open door as she grasped the *barre* with both her hands and raised her right leg in a controlled, liquid motion. Her pointed toe climbed toward the ceiling as smoothly as if it were riding an elevator.

What a woman. For just a blink in eternity's eye, she'd been his.

Strength, beauty, and extreme flexibility aside—and shame on him for never pinning her leg behind her head like that in bed—losing the

Monticello opportunity was not an option. He needed her. She'd have to come around. And quickly.

She struck him with a calm, cool stare, as if challenging his last thought. A hint of a smile touched her lips, but vanished with her next breath.

In tribute to their past, he brushed a kiss onto two fingers and wiggled them in her direction. "Until we meet again," he whispered.

"In hell," she mouthed in return.

*   *   *

Star's fingers smoothed up the sides of wet clay, forming a large crock on the potter's wheel. Over the years, her basement art room, warm with the heat of a kiln and pure with the scent of terra cotta, had become a refuge, a place to sort through the things she inexplicably knew. She didn't question her gift the way Molly did, and she didn't block it the way Brandywine chose to.

She'd come from a long line of mystics, each of whom had come into a unique talent at an opportune moment in her life. And the pain of losing her husband was a small price to pay for her sixth sense. Men flitted in and out of a woman's life, but a girl's aptitude for the unexplained remained hers forever. Star knew things without possessing reason for knowing them. It seemed as normal to her as gravy on mashed potatoes.

Take the stranger in front of the Dance Connection, for example. She'd never laid eyes on him before, but she knew for certain he'd traveled a great distance, and he'd come for Molly.

A handsome man with sinful green eyes, he looked as if carried the weight of the world on his broad shoulders. Something tragic lurked in his past, something that had made him a man when other boys his age concentrated on baseball games and homecoming dates. He'd begun to have nightmares about it again.

The clay slipped through Star's fingers, malleable and submissive. Nothing like her feisty niece, who could surely give this stranger a run for his money, if only she'd release the indigo and cobalt in her core center.

For the past few days, Star couldn't look at the girl without seeing it. The colors should have represented celebration, but something had gone terribly awry.

Somehow, this man had stolen Molly's appetite—for food, for passion. Now that he'd returned, without a doubt, he would feed her, and whether he knew it or not, he needed her as much as she needed him.

*   *   *

Humidity hung heavy in the air, covering Molly with a chilled, uncomfortable mist the moment she exited the dance studio. She pulled her short trench coat around her and walked westward down Center Street.

It was diabolical, Scott Sheridan appearing at the studio door, just when she couldn't chase him out of her mind, coming to her after a five-year absence, looking at her as if he wanted to peel off her clothing and have his husbandly way with her. Such an incredible twist of fate, and premonitions weren't even her *modus operandi*.

Scott had taken her on a tour of Jeffersonian homes shortly after they'd married. She'd never felt as alive as when she'd felt uncertain energy at those old homes, and Scott seemed intrigued—if not baffled—with her mysterious faculty. And he'd sparked something deep inside her again, just by showing his handsome face in Parker's Landing.

His hard, brawny chest hadn't softened one iota. His green eyes weren't any less mesmerizing either, which meant his adept hands would probably be just as skilled, slowly working their way over her—

The studio door slammed behind her, and she flinched.

"Wait up, girlfriend."

Molly stopped at the cobblestone corner of Center and Whitney and turned toward her cousin. "I don't want to talk about it."

"So I gather." Brandywine hooked an arm around her shoulders. "What gives?"

"Shellshock, that's what."

"He's one hunk of a shell."

"Oh, he's gorgeous. I'll give you that one."

Brandywine massaged her chin, mocking deep thought. "Yeah, I'm afraid I'm going to need a little more."

"What do you want me to say?"

"For starters, when? When did all this happen?"

"Five years ago. I met him at a lecture in Virginia, married him six days later, and just when we were on our way here to announce our marriage, he served me with divorce papers, in front of Marc Chagall's *America Windows*."

"Ooh, *America Windows*. Star was right about the blue."

"Forget the blue." Molly pulled free. "He left me for Thomas Jefferson, and suddenly—"

"He left you for a dead president?"

"Focus."

"Believe me, I'm trying." She fished through her dance bag. "I'm going to call Aunt Dusky."

"I don't believe in psychic massage."

"At the very least, you'll get a long-overdue rub-down, but mark my words, this is a delicious situation. A six-day courtship turned marriage. And now he's back. Wonder what it means?"

"Nothing." Molly sliced the heavy air with a horizontal motion of her hand.

"Then why did he show up at dance class?" Brandywine flipped open her phone. "You were destined to meet him, destined to marry him. Destined to part until this moment right here. He wants to rekindle the flame."

Molly pulled the trench tighter. "Doubtful. One call from Professor Wilkinson about some unearthed book sent him packing. Men who choose moldy, musty books over their wives *never* want to rekindle flames."

"Then why is he on your steps?" Phone at her ear, Brandywine nodded to the right.

"Tell me it isn't true." Molly forced herself to look across Park Avenue at the beige painted lady with a signature red door.

And he was there, all right, sitting on her porch, his feet resting on the fifth stair. Small, round glasses perched before his emerald eyes as he read a paperback, humid wind tousling his hopelessly satiny black hair. She forced her mouth to close, but was powerless to turn away from the vision of six-feet-two-inches of Man huddled on her porch like a homeward-bound puppy.

A thick, cream-colored sweater stretched across his broad chest as if it were made to showcase his pectorals, and his masculine fingers turned pages with a motion reminiscent of his caress on her naked back.

For twenty-nine days he'd known just what to do with his hands at just the right time. Hands in her hair, thumbs tracing her lips, an index finger trailing along her inner thigh. She shivered and, entranced with memories, inched toward him.

They'd trespassed on plantation grounds. The natural scent of the Virginia soil, red like winter wheat, had reminded her of growth, of destiny. His nimble fingers had worked the zipper on her skirt, then the buttons on her blouse, with painstaking patience. He'd nudged a knee between her legs, cupped her rear in his capable hands, and tickled the lace tops of her thigh-high stockings. *Leave them on.*

She'd peeled his trousers from his lean hips, dipped a hand into his cotton boxer shorts, and found him hard. Heard him groan with the first stroke.

With a deep thrust, he'd plunged into her body, and their flesh melded beneath the stars just south of the honeymoon gazebo.

Ah, Monticello.

So far away, so long ago.

And yet, here and now.

The scent of familiar cologne drifted on the wet breeze, and she blinked when he took her hand. "Scottie."

He looked up at her and smiled with straight, white teeth. "Hey, cupcake."

Molly maneuvered her hand from his grasp and paced up the stairs, forging a path around her ex-husband, as if he were an object she'd forgotten to stow. *To Do List: Clear a space in the attic for a breathing statue of my ex-husband.* "How did you know this was my place?"

"Your last name's plastered on your mailbox."

And repaint the mailbox.

"She's talking to you, Molly."

"What?" She blinked into his steady, sparkling gaze.

"Your friend." He hitched his chin toward the street.

"Brandywine's my cousin."

"Your cousin." He smiled. "Family."

"Yes, I have a family."

"Aunt Dusky can squeeze you in tomorrow at six," Brandywine called from the sidewalk, turning toward Westerfield Place. "Be there."

"I don't need a massage," Molly called to Brandywine's back.

"Someone ought to rub you right." Scott grinned, fanning through the pages of his paperback. "Ever read this one? It's probably the best historical fiction I've read about Sally Hemings."

She ignored the novel—and the deliciously thick finger tucked into it—shouldered past him to the door, and turned the finicky knob...to no avail. "Some might argue that Jefferson's concubine slave is hardly fictitious." She again turned the knob, this time slamming her hip against the door, but still it didn't open. "Great timing, Gracie."

With a smooth motion, he reached over her arm and placed his hand atop hers on the antique brass doorknob. *Warm. Strong. Enticing.*

12

"Some might say there's truth to Miss Hemings, but that doesn't mean every word written about her is true." He twisted the knob, and the door opened.

"Thank you." She stepped onto the hardwood floor in her foyer, the original fir of 1896, sanded and finished in a deep sienna stain with stenciled ivy along the perimeter. A delightful welcome mat, if she did say so, herself.

"Who's Gracie?" he asked, pulling the glasses from the bridge of his nose and tucking them into the collar of his sweater. "A roommate?"

"Who?"

"You said 'Great timing, Gracie.'"

"I did?" *I did.* She clenched her teeth, pulled the coat from her body, and hung it in the Chippendale wardrobe she'd recently refinished. "Gracie's my ghost."

He cracked a smile. "Your ghost?"

"I grew up in this creaky, old house. Whenever something sticks, I blame it on Gracie."

"Not on your inability to work simple ergonomic tools like window latches, shower faucets, and door knobs?" He grinned again.

"I'm not clumsy."

"Obviously. I've recently seen you on a dance floor. How long have you been dancing like that?"

"My whole life."

"When I knew you?"

"Evidence that we don't know each other, Scott. Not well enough to dive into the sacred institution of marriage, and not well enough for you to assess my downfalls with 'simple ergonomic tools,' about which, by the way, you're wrong."

"Really? If you're so good with house keys, why don't you lock your door?"

"Welcome to Parker's Landing. I know the mailman's middle name, for crying out loud."

"The mailman's middle name." He bounced the paperback against his palm. "Well, pray tell. What is it?"

She drew in a long, cleansing breath, trying not to look at his hands, trying to forget their powers of persuasion. "What are you doing here, Scottie?"

"I'd like to come in past the threshold and close the door, if you don't mind. It's cold outside."

"What do you expect when you don't wear a jacket?"

"I expect you might need some warming up, yourself." His gaze shifted from her eyes to her breasts, then back again.

Head-to-toe in pink Lycra-spandex, she crossed her arms over her chest, hiding her perked nipples. She kicked the black leather clogs from her bare feet, and although she nodded toward the parlor, inviting her ex-husband in, she didn't step aside.

He smiled again, this time without sarcasm, and for a torrential moment, she longed to see him through the eyes of the twenty-three-year-old girl who had fallen for him. Simple, pure lust. *And, oh, to give into it again...*

He closed the door, inching toward her. "You look incredible, cupcake."

And when he said things like that, her heartbeat became a cacophony in her ears. He was close enough to hear it. *Could he?* God, she hoped not. He shouldn't know he could turn her to butter after all this time, but those eyes, that drawl...

"More than incredible," he said.

"You, too," she whispered.

He brushed the spine of the book against her chin. "I bought it at that charming used book store in town."

His eyes hypnotized her, and she felt as if she were falling into them, spiraling into the depths of his soul. Suddenly, she couldn't recall her own middle name, let alone the mailman's. Scott was taking her hand and licking his lips, and—

"I bought it for you." He placed the worn book into her hand. "Just after I met the captain of the Vintage Car Club at Charlie's. Great guy. Says the fishing's better than I might expect in Gray's Lake."

She blinked her gaze away from his lips, only to continue the affair with his eyes.

"Molly?"

"Yes?"

"Can I come in?"

You can come anywhere you want.

14

CHAPTER 2

"Well, can I?" With a jolt of a smile, he closed her hands around the endearing book.

Come inside. Please, I need it. She blinked. "Of course," she said, sounding more breathless than she cared to admit. She led him between a pair of paneled pocket doors, so heavy they always stood open, and into the parlor.

"Mind if I close these?" How could he sound so nonchalant? So casual? "That foyer of yours is drafty."

"Actually, I—"

"Gracie again?"

"I like them open."

"Because you can't close them?"

She perched her hands on her hips, straightening. "What's it to you anyway?"

He grasped a glass doorknob in each hand, effortlessly closed the pocket doors, and turned toward her, a long, lascivious gaze lingering on her legs. "You know, I wouldn't mind flying up here every now and then to close or open them at your whim."

"I think I might find someone more qualified for the task. But thanks for the offer." She tossed the book—such a thoughtful gift— onto the cherry Queen Anne butler's tray she used in lieu of a coffee table, when all she really wanted to do was hold the paperback tight to her chest. *Lucky pages, having basked in the pleasure of his touch.*

"Nice piece."

Of ass? She whipped her head toward him. "Crude, even for—"

He trailed a finger along the top of the butler's tray.

"Oh. It's a replica. I was out-bid for the antique one I found at an estate auction, but it makes the necessary statement."

"Indeed." He sank onto an early 1800s Duncan-Phyfe sofa, with the original cranberry velvet upholstering. She'd discovered it at a garage sale last year.

Such a steal. She couldn't prove it, but with her heightened sense, she knew it had been made for a diplomat in Philadelphia.

"And since I'm not qualified for"—he gave her a quick head-to-toe once-over—"other things, how about a drink?"

She tossed her dance bag over her shoulder and eyed him, wanting to straddle him where he sat, despite the historical significance of the furniture. "I've got a bottle of merlot. But you'll have to open it."

"Of course. Gracie's a bitch with that cork screw, isn't she?"

"And that sofa's really just to look at, so if you don't mind..." She waved him along.

*   *   *

He rose from the sofa, careful not to put too much weight on any one section, cautious with his hands. He should've known not to sit on an antique. Well, that was the problem actually. He couldn't decipher what was original and what wasn't. That's why he needed her. Well, he needed her for other things, too. Her intuition—and her long legs— were unparalleled in the academic community.

"The University of Virginia has an original Duncan Phyfe sofa," she said, leading him through an arched opening to a large, red-walled dining room furnished with an impressive table set for twelve, with an embroidered, ivory table cloth spread beneath blue-and-white plates. "Did you know that?"

"Know what?"

"About the Duncan Phyfe."

"No. Who in their right mind would?"

"A Jeffersonian historian."

"Are you expecting company?"

"No, why?"

"The dishes, the tablecloth..." He reached out to touch a plate. *So delicate, so detailed.*

"They aren't dishes. They're Wedgwood china. A family heirloom recently passed to me. It's the same pattern found at Mary

Washington's house."

He pulled his hand away a split second before his fingers met the china. *Whew. Close one.*

"My mother wanted to give them to me as a wedding gift, but since she doesn't think I'll ever get married, she—"

"Again." He touched her elbow. "Married again."

She turned toward him, a look of solemn grace in her eyes. "Excuse me?"

"You've been married. To me."

"That wasn't a marriage, Scott. That was an annoying draw of the deck. 'Hearts, we get married.' What kind of a proposal was that?"

"I'd have married you, no matter what suit I drew. But as it turned out, I drew the ten of hearts, so you never knew that."

"Is that right? What card did you draw when you decided to divorce me?"

"What we had didn't last long, Molly, but it was real." His fingers, burning from the addictive feel of her skin, slid from her flesh. "Why do you think I opted for divorce? Because an annulment would have meant we were false, nonexistent."

"Should I be flattered that we were real? That you chose to divorce me, instead of annulling me? For the sake of Jefferson's boyhood journal found on the grounds of Tuckahoe plantation?"

He ached to explain it all, to admit he'd used the journal as an excuse to leave—because he couldn't bear the thought of her knowing the real reason. "There were circumstances, demands. Reasons I had to follow the lead, and reasons for you to stay here."

"What circumstance could possibly surpass the reality of our marriage? What reasons could you possibly fathom that might override the way I feel—the way I *felt*—about you?"

"We were real." He brushed a soft curl from her forehead. "So real."

"Is that right?" She caught his hand before it fell to his side, her thumb massaging his ring finger at a crucial location. "All evidence points to the contrary, professor." The thud of her dance bag against the hardwood floors punctuated the anger in her eyes.

"I need you."

"You need my knowledge of period pieces."

"Whatever."

"'Whatever?' Are Jefferson's memoirs 'whatever' to you? I'm a historian, too, you know, with a concentration important enough to bring you halfway across the country to my doorstep. I advise you to watch your tone, Dr. Sheridan. That 'whatever' is my livelihood."

"And I advise you to follow your destiny, Miss Molly. It's just like you're always saying: things happen for a reason."

"I can't believe you're quoting the doctrine of predestination. Whatever happened to Manifest Destiny?"

"I'm making my own way." He shoved his hands into his pockets. "And if I have to use your philosophy to do so, I'll do it. This is too important, Molly."

Her cheeks flushed a crimson red, and a fire sparked in her eyes. "You."

He shrugged a shoulder. "And you, Molly. We're too good a team to—"

"You used my philosophy against me five years ago, too. At Christ's Church in Alexandria. We were destined to draw that card, you said. Why delay the inevitable, you said."

"I don't assume anything is predetermined, but I rationalized having you as my right."

"You were wrong about me. Then and now." She spun like a miniscule tornado and shot between a pair of doors, each about eighteen inches wide, wavy glass inserts reflecting her dancer's figure. "You have no rights stamped on this body. You can't claim someone like land. I'm not the Louisiana Purchase."

"Actually, we paid for the Louisiana Territory. Hence the 'purchase' in its name, although it was quite a bargain." He followed her into the kitchen, where, in silence, she placed a corkscrew, a dusty bottle of wine, and a single glass atop a work table in the center of the room, before heading back the way they'd come.

"Aren't you going to join me?" he asked.

"Who says that glass is for you? It might take me half the night, but I'll manage to open that bottle if I have to crack it against the bathtub."

"Molly." He started after her. "Molly, wait. Let's talk. Lord knows we never did."

"You waited five years to decide just how to drop in on me. Give me five seconds to decide how to kick you out."

"Molly!"

She rushed through the dining room and entered the parlor, glaring back at him. "How dare you come to me after all this time, repentant only when an apology might help your career?"

"Molly, wait." He fought a smile. She was cute when she was mad.

Always had been. "I can't go. I don't know the mailman's middle name yet."

She tugged on the pocket doors, but they didn't budge. "Do you even know my middle name, Scottie?" She grasped one knob with both hands and thrust the weight of her entire body toward the pocket. The door scraped open an inch. "Because I took the time to learn your name in its entirety." She tugged again. "I wanted to know everything about you, but you very obviously aren't interested in knowing me."

If she only knew how hard it had been to say goodbye.

Tug, tug, tug.

He reached for her, gently pulling her by the arm, struggling to make—and keep—eye contact.

"I leave these doors open for a reason, Nathaniel Scott Sheridan, the Fourth"—

He pinned her wrists to the doors and drew in a nose full of lilac.

—"and I like them open. This is my—"

He kissed her words away, imprisoning her against the ornately carved wood. "Yeah, well, I like them closed," he said against her lips.

She gasped into his mouth—"You son of a..."—kissing him in return. One long leg wrapped around him, pulling him closer still, pressing her pelvis to his hardening sex.

Damn, she felt good. And he needed to feel more.

He released her wrists and trailed his hand along the leg enfolding him. With gentle pressure, he eased it higher and higher, resting her ankle on his shoulder. He could feel all of her now. The breasts that filled not more than his palms. The nipples he'd once drizzled in hot fudge. The flat stomach he'd taken great pleasure in navigating with his tongue. The opening between her thighs and the hidden button he knew how to push until her eyes welled with tears of pleasure.

His hands wandered, feeling every inch of her body, only the thin material of a dancer's garment standing in his way. He caressed his way to the back of the leotard and pulled her a fraction of an inch off the door, his fingers sauntering up her strong back. Did she still purr like a kitten with the slightest caress up her spine?

A throaty sigh against his lips confirmed his musings. Some things—like her last name—had changed over the past five years. But he suspected those primal sounds would remain with her always.

He drew a line along the scoop neck of the leotard with a sudden urge to rip it from her body and feel her naked flesh, to give her the orgasm he'd been dreaming of since he'd left her standing at those intriguing blue windows so many years ago.

Her muscled rear tensed beneath his squeezing fingers, making him even more aware of her strength, her definition, and the fact she wasn't wearing panties. *Oh, Lord.*

Such a beautiful woman. And he had her up against the door, legs in a vertical split and her body encapsulated with his hands like bookends. "Molly."

Her eyes flickered open, steam exuding from her split-second stare, before falling closed again with his next kiss.

The thin garment did little to hide her every curve, but revealing as it was, it stood like a fortress between them, his hands no match for its guard. "I can't find an opening anywhere in this damn thing."

*   *   *

He surrounded her with virility, awakening her body and tickling her soul. His swift hands—she remembered they'd traveled fast, on agendas all their own—seared against her, enticing her to let go of the anger, let go of the blue. Lose herself in the pleasure he was sure to provide.

She tingled in anticipation she hadn't felt in years and ached to feel him throbbing inside her. They'd been magical together, that's for sure. She'd never understood the spontaneous combustion, but a passionate flame had engulfed her the moment Scott had kissed her the first time. His touch had been electrifying, and she'd welcomed every second of it, acted on impulse, followed an urge too incredible to ignore.

Much like she was doing now.

She trembled, knowing where this path would lead. History was sure to repeat itself if they continued. And as much as she pined to feel the magic again, she knew the sullen ache of its fading. She couldn't go through it again. Couldn't and wouldn't, no matter how great his hands felt on her body.

She reached for a doorknob to stabilize the rambunctious tremors within her. Once her hand met the glass knob, she grasped it tightly, praying for the strength to deny him. But his mouth moved over hers as if it were designed to kiss her, and the lingering taste of cinnamon on his tongue left her nostalgic.

He'd left sticks of cinnamon chewing gum in his pockets on every—all right, on the three—occasions she'd done his laundry. At the time, it had irritated her, but now she found comfort in the intimate knowledge, found peace in knowing she held something sacred in her heart.

However briefly, she'd been his wife. No other woman on the face of the planet could put that on her resumé. And if his pulsing cock pressing against her were any indication, he was ready to treat her the way men traditionally treated wives. *To Do List: Sex Scott goodbye.*

What harm could come of their making love one last time? He wasn't a random man. He was a man she had married, and they deserved a chance to say goodbye, didn't they? They'd certainly never given themselves the chance five years—

The door gave way beneath her hand, zipping like lightning into the pocket.

She gasped in surprise, but Scott tightened his grip, saving her from a certain fall, without so much as breaking their kiss.

"Great timing, Gracie," he whispered with a smile, resting his forehead against hers.

His hands remained where he'd planted them—one on her rear and the other between her shoulder blades—burning through her leotard. She lifted her leg from his shoulder and lowered it to the ground with learned discipline.

"When the Jeffries not to be confused with the Jefferson—family donated the Duncan Phyfe to the University of Virginia in 1976, it was a bordeaux velvet. Probably similar to mine." She attempted to step back, prying at his hands, but he held her stationary.

"Tell me about the couch later." He leaned in to kiss her again, but she turned her cheek to him at the last minute.

"Not a couch. A Duncan Phyfe sofa."

"We've still got it, cupcake," he whispered, nibbling a wet kiss onto her lobe. "You feel it, too."

"I've just come from class. I have to ..." She looked to him again. "I should freshen up."

His gaze trailed to the pile of hair atop her head. "Why do you always wear it up?"

"It gets in the way, but I'm afraid to chop it any shorter."

"Why not wear a ponytail?"

"Too long for dance class."

"May I?" he asked.

She blinked. He wanted to take her hair down. "Scottie, I don't think—"

"You and I both know if I'm not touching your hair, I'll find something else to touch. So what's it going to be? Your body or your hair?"

"It isn't as long as it used to be."

"From the looks of it, there's still plenty up there." He pulled a hairpin loose. "How many am I looking for?"

"Scottie, I don't think—"

"How many more?" His eyes were green embers, fixated on her lips, as if waiting for them to move. She might've melted beneath the heat of his scrutiny, but she couldn't budge. "Molly?"

"Twenty."

"One." He plucked another pin and pressed a sweet kiss onto her forehead. "Two." He nibbled her chin. "Three." Left eyelid. "Four." His tongue melted against her right inner wrist, his lips massaging her tender flesh, awakening nerves she'd forgotten existed.

Oh, no. She was in trouble now.

* * *

"Five."

Her steady gaze bored into his with the intensity of a thousand suns, and her lips parted. Kiss number five landed precisely on those hot, luscious lips, parlaying into kisses six, seven, and eight. To account for them, he felt for and pulled three more pins from her bun.

"Nine," he breathed onto her neck, rolling his tongue against her peachy skin. Nine hairpins found a home in his left pocket clanging against her orphaned wedding band, and he plucked ten, eleven, twelve, thirteen, and fourteen pins out, a garland of kisses trailing from one side of her neck to the other.

Auburn tresses draped about her face. "Lord, you look romantic as hell," he whispered, fingering a soft curl. "Fifteen." He lowered his mouth to the hollow of her collarbone, tasting a trace of salty sweat from her workout, and found another pin.

"We won't make it to twenty." She sounded desperate for him to stop, but eager for him to continue.

What to do, what to do? What did she want? He inched away— better safe than sorry—but she held him fast. Her fingers laced into his hair, and she hungrily bit into his lips.

He tried to hide the satisfied smile creeping upon him. "Sixteen." Scott kissed her shoulder, his tongue bleeding moisture through the thin leotard. He trailed the bunch of pins across a distended nipple—a lovely gasp of surprised pleasure rewarded him—over her concave belly, and dropped them into his pocket.

"Seventeen," she said in a rushed whisper.

He dove his hands into her mass of hair, his fingers rubbing her scalp, frantically searching for the pin she'd already called out. "Seventeen." He inched it from its confines and twirled it between his fingers.

Their gazes locked, and she licked her lips, staring at his mouth. *No, Molly. Not on the mouth. Not this time.* He divided his attention between her beautiful face and the breast he was suddenly cupping. He traced her nipple with his thumb, gauged her uneven inhalations, and lowered his mouth to her breast.

"Scottie." She tensed against him with hurried, spoken encouragement.

The lace of the bra beneath her dancewear tantalized his tongue, and memories of her lingerie-clad body twisted among linens in his mind.

The eighteenth pin tangled in her hair, and she gasped, when he pulled it free. "Careful."

He yanked another, again kissing her breast. He hadn't tongued such a perfect specimen in—

"What number was that?" Her breathless words sounded as if in a cloud, jarring him from what seemed an idyllic dream. "Scottie?"

"Nineteen."

"Get on with it already."

Indeed. If only he could find the last hairpin... He delved into her long hair, searching, stroking, remembering the feel of those locks drifting across his bare chest. *Have to feel that again. Screw number twenty.* With or without it, they were ready. Primed. He dipped his hand to the warmth between her legs—

"Oh."

—and devoured her mouth, drinking from her, feeding her.

The pin shook free of its own accord and dropped to the hardwood floor.

He massaged her externally, wanting to tear the leotard to shreds and bury himself raw into her depths. To feel her strong, wet insides working his cock.

"Scottie." She tightened her grip on his shoulders, pressed her torso to his, and dragged her tongue along the underside of his.

He shuddered with pleasure—was anything hotter than a woman licking his mouth in prelude?—and pulled at her clothes. "Lord, I've missed you."

"What?"

"I've." Kiss. "Missed." Kiss. "You."

"Don't say that."

"I've missed you."

"Don't say things you don't mean."

He buried his mouth in the crook of her neck, inhaling the lilac scent of her hair. "It's true."

"Stop it." Two small hands pressed at his chest and shoved him an inch or two away. The sultry desire in her eyes was no match for the fiery anger creeping in. Nothing a great kiss couldn't fix with any normal woman, but with Molly... "Stop."

He took a step back, shoving his hands through his hair. "You're the last thing I deserve right now."

All too much, too soon.

"I'll just be a minute." She backed into the foyer toward the staircase, her hair a long, sweeping mess that reached to the middle of her back and hung in her eyes, as rumpled as if she'd just rolled out of bed. "Can you give me a minute?"

The weighted clock in Monticello's entrance hall, Jefferson's own invention, appeared in his mind. Time was a precious entity. He had little of it in this race to win the opportunity of his career, and he'd already wasted five crucial years of what could have been his future. An irrational image materialized of little boys racing around Washington and Lee campus, awaiting him, playing tag, tackling their mother on the quad, her long, auburn hair floating on the sweet Virginia breeze.

"Just a minute, all right?" Her delicate hand trailed along the curve of a railing, and she disappeared up the stairs.

He slipped a hand into his pocket, fingering the ring, jingling the hairpins. No, he couldn't give her a minute. Not when he wanted once again to demand the rest of her life.

What he needed was a long, cool shower...and not the kind that involved imprisoning a shivering ex-wife against cold tile and warming her with fiery kisses. He needed to wash away the fulfillment she'd briefly provided against the double pocket doors, and—yes—during their marriage; to get out before he began to believe all things were possible with love.

He couldn't welcome her into his world again; it would be too risky, too dangerous. Regardless of whatever she'd felt for him five years ago—whatever she felt now—her feelings would surely change the moment she realized the truth behind his mother's death. And she'd do so the moment she set foot on Honey Hill, his family's estate. Would it have been easier, had he known of her eerie talent before they'd married? Maybe then, he wouldn't have popped the question.

Ha! As if the magic between them had ever been a choice! As if he ever could have denied it! He'd been a fool to assume their energy would've waned over the years, and should've anticipated it only would've grown. Wasn't he in a pickle now? He needed her help, but more pressing was a need of a basic nature. He needed the one woman who could easily decipher his long-hidden secret, and thus, the one woman he should never bring home.

He strolled past the couch—*er, sofa*—and pocketed the discarded paperback. Such a stupid idea, thinking he could win her help with a probably false tale of love between Jefferson and Hemings. Such a brazen assumption that he could again ignore the feelings Molly stirred in him. The only way to ignore it was to bury it as deeply as he'd interred his secret, and if he expected to keep it from her, while winning the opportunity of a lifetime, he'd have to pile the dirt high.

He inched through the dining room, past the heirloom Wedgwood, and into the kitchen, where he cut the foil from the lonely bottle of merlot. Soft steps of a dancer's feet ceased above him, replaced with the rush of a tub faucet and the whistle of a train approaching the Parker's Landing Metra station.

He opened the bottle of wine, poured a glass, and did the hardest thing he'd ever done. Again. But this time, he wouldn't have the strength to stay away, and he wouldn't have a random book to use an excuse.

CHAPTER 3

The heat of Scott's hands remained on Molly's flesh, despite her attempts to scrub it away. Addictive. Necessary. And only one level below her, offering not only a surefire release of pleasure, but a chance to launch her career into something much more noteworthy than estate auctions and appraisals.

Submerged in her vintage Victorian soaker tub with her recently liberated hair tied in a haphazard ponytail, she squeezed a drenched sponge over her body. Lilac-scented bubbles trickled over her breasts, caressing their way down her belly—she did *not* look too thin—and tickled between her legs. Why did she have to want him?

He'd made his choice the minute Wilkinson had requested his help with that damn journal, and he hadn't chosen Molly. She was a glutton for punishment to even consider wanting him now.

She propped her feet on the porcelain edge, surrendering to the water's buoyancy. Her hips rose to the height of the water, reminding her of Scott's natural ability to manipulate her body, to position and reposition her.

Where was he anyway? He never could resist interrupting her baths, and she'd been certain he'd join her…if only to discuss the Monticello opportunity. But her requested minute had long since come and gone, and she was starting to think he'd found a conscience during their time apart.

Well, if he wasn't coming, she wasn't soaking herself into a prune waiting for him. She rose from the tub, her thighs jiggling against the water. Would any exercise pare down the bulk of once-muscular legs? *To Do List: Curse my lifelong commitment to dance and the thighs that come with it.*

Her old, white robe fit the contour of her body with comfort, much like her ex-husband. *Damn him and his perfect hands.* She yanked her hair free from the scrunchy. And after their thorough preheating against the pocket doors, he didn't even have the decency to barge into her bathroom while she was nude.

Fine. If he'd come for an adult conversation about Jefferson's beloved plantation, that's what he'd get. That and nothing else.

Besides, he'd always said she was prettiest when rumpled and wearing comfortable clothes. She could make this the most lustful, tempting conversation about work he'd ever had. Far more alluring than Wilkinson and that ratty, old book she'd found. Ooh, wouldn't it just nab him in the 'nads if she waltzed downstairs in one of his old, forgotten shirts, one she'd tossed on after a long night of mind-bending sex in Alexandria.

Perfect. She opened a creaking door and climbed fourteen steep steps to the attic studio, where she danced Fridays through Wednesdays, and whenever class wasn't in session. At the far end of the attic was a walk-in closet, where she'd stashed mementos from her youth, including a loaded hatbox in which she'd kept all things related to Professor Scott Sheridan: a romantic sonnet, with which he'd declared his love for her the day after they'd met; the white babydoll nightgown she'd worn the night they'd married; her copy of their divorce papers.

Jeez, where was it?

For an impatient man who hadn't waited more than an hour into their first meeting to kiss her, he was certainly waiting quietly downstairs for her. What was he waiting for?

Boxes of old dance shoes, dollhouse furniture, old family photos. No hatbox of sinful memories. She shoved hair from her eyes, her throat suddenly as arid as Arizona. Where was it? It had to be there somewhere. She'd moved it to another closet, that's all. But she still had it, right? It was still there, as close to her body as was her heart. Right?

Her search traveled to the highest shelf, her hand feeling for what would be too high to see. *Please, please, please.*

The closet door squeaked behind her, the cluttered, narrow space growing more and more dim, and then the door closed with a snap.

"Gracie!" She kicked the door back open and took a deep breath, emerging from the confines of the overstocked closet to the tranquil sunset filtering through the semi-circular window in the highest gable. "All right, all right, you've convinced me. I'll look for it later."

A tingling sensation darted through her ribcage, one that reminded her of making out in corners of dark rooms. If Scott would do his job and interrupt her, perhaps they'd put the studio to use in an interesting manner. The maple floors would be far from cozy against her back, but the room reeked of passion. Always had. With or without the company of Scott Sheridan.

She walked down the first flight of stairs. After a quick peek in a wavy mirror, and a dusting of powder to camouflage her freckles, she pattered down the second flight, a nervous fluttering in her stomach. "So tell me more about this project."

No answer.

"Scott?" She alit from the staircase and headed toward her front room. "I'm sorry to keep you waiting, but—"

The book he'd given her. It was gone.

"Scottie?"

She traveled through the dining room and great room, peeked into the library. No sign of him, and the powder room door stood open, negating the possibility of his detainment there. He'd left. And he'd taken back the most thoughtful part of his visit, too, the dirty rat.

With clenched teeth, and a touch of embarrassment at fussing over her appearance for a once-again-absent man, she swung through the mullioned doors to the kitchen. And stopped suddenly.

A lone glass of red wine stood amid the pile of today's—all right, and yesterday's—mail. One envelope was propped against the bottle, Scott's blue-penciled scratch of penmanship warming a piece of her heart. He'd scrawled her a sonnet in blue pencil, too. It was his preferred medium for grading student essays. Not as messy as red ink, he'd said.

Miss Molly, have a drink for me. When you're ready to talk, give a call. (I'm borrowing your car. Impossible to get a cab in this town.) My love to Gracie.

A phone number dared her, as if blinking in neon pink. She picked up the telephone and dialed. After four rings, she was about to hang up, but finally…

"Hello."

"Brandy."

"Oh, thank God you called. What happened? Is he still there? Did you—"

"Can you give me a lift to work tomorrow? He took my car."

"He stole your car?"

"No, he borrowed it while I was in the tub, probably so I'd have to call him."

"So, call him."

"Will you shut up and get over here? I need you."

She pictured her cousin worrying over her thumbnail in the silence that followed.

"Brandywine Alexandra, get over here."

"I don't know, Mol. He seems worth a conversation—"

"I'll expect you in five minutes."

"Molly, wait. Star says I shouldn't intervene with destiny."

"Since when do you do everything your mother says? I bailed you out of more than one rebellion in your teens, remember. You owe me."

"Okay, I'll come over. But just to drop off Star's monstrous dinner plate."

"I'll see you in five."

Four-and-a-half minutes later, Brandywine clattered a foil-wrapped half loaf of bread and a platter of roast beef, steamed sugar snap peas, and wild rice onto the countertop. Enough food for at least three grown men. "*Bon appetit.*"

"I don't know how either of you expects me to eat."

"Some people eat through crises." Brandywine pulled a pink beret from her mop of curls and perched on a stool next to the work table. "Proof of the pudding, literally—my ass."

"I'd kill for your bod."

"No need for murder, just eat. And I'm instructed to watch you, so make it quick. I've got a date tonight."

"New guy?" Molly pulled the foil from the platter and a mouth-watering aroma steamed toward her. *Mmmm. Just a bite maybe.* She grabbed a fork and knife.

"Nice penmanship." Brandywine fingered Scott's note. "Screams 'doctor.'"

"He has a doctorate in American History. Teaches at Washington and Lee."

"Listen, maybe it hurts you to see him. Maybe you don't deserve the pain, but we don't always have a choice about these things."

Molly shrugged, shoveling a forkful of rice into her mouth. "Maybe

I'm meant to learn from him. Yada, yada, yada. Spare me the lecture. I was raised with the same doctrines—and until you were seven, under the same roof."

"Hey, take this out on Mr. *America Windows*. I'm just here to compile a report on your consumption for my mother. And, while we're on the subject, what do you weigh? A buck-o-five?"

Molly shrugged, swiping a napkin over her lips. The last time she'd stepped on a scale, she'd weighed ten pounds more than her cousin's guess, and thus, she'd thrown the scale against the wall and broken it.

"This isn't about just you, Mol. People care about you. And at five-six, you should weigh at least—"

"I'm not trying to starve. I'm just not hungry."

"Well, get hungry. You look like a twig, and anyone too thin to menstruate has a problem." Brandywine took the phone and dialed.

"Don't call Star. I'm eating."

Brandywine raised a brow, looking like a younger, thinner version of her mother, and slipped from the stool. "I'm going to get ready for my date. Let me know how it goes with the mysterious ex."

"I'm not calling him."

"Too late." Brandywine pushed the speaker phone button and grinned, wiggling her fingers in a goodbye wave.

*   *   *

Scott stretched his tired body on the lumpy mattress in room twelve. *Not bad for a seedy motel actually.* He'd stayed in much worse. Always dark and sultry, rooms like this one had histories all their own. Usually of the unforgiving, hard-sex variety. He'd never had Molly in a room of this character, but Lord, he'd love to pin her up against a mangy wall, one of her ankles resting on his shoulder, the other leg wrapped around his waist. Shove her skirt up her thighs, and rip her tiny panties to shreds. Ram into her depths, while she nipped at his mouth in hungry, uncontrolled kisses, her hair spilling all around her flushed face.

Oh, what a picture of perfection—her classy, if not pristine, posture a paradox against the crumbling surroundings. There was a certain challenge in pleasuring a woman without touching the bed or the floor...

The national anthem chimed from the bedside table—his cell phone, in dire need of a change in ring tones. A Pavlovian gear inside his head urged him to stand every time he heard it, but such wasn't possible in traffic jams—or when thoughts of Molly and sub-par oases occupied things below his belt. Humiliating, really, that mere musings could arouse him, as if he were thirteen again. He brought the phone to his ear. "Yeah."

"Brandywine," Molly hissed.

He felt a smile coming on, and the member in his khakis grew another fraction. "Guess again, cupcake."

"Where are you, and where's my car?"

"With me. At Rohde's Inn."

"The fleabag on the way to the interstate?"

"Are you offering something more respectable?"

"Somehow, our shacking up doesn't ring 'respectable,' now does it?"

He stared at the flaking popcorn ceiling above him. *No.* Their near-sex earlier that evening didn't rate as reputable. "It was good to see you, Molly."

"Like no time had passed at all." A long, slow breath fuzzed through the phone. "But let's not talk about it now. Tell me about this Monticello gig."

A warm sensation shimmied through him. He had her now, if only for the history of Jefferson's sacred plot of land.

"I mean, why, Scott? Why me?"

"You don't know?"

"I think there's someone out there with an east coast education you might prefer."

"I think you have to do this—"

"I think you're grasping at straws."

"—because it's your destiny." *And mine.*

"How do you figure?"

"You're an excellent historian. And true, there are many intelligent folks in Virginia who know what you do about furniture. But you have a gift to capture the feeling of a room like no one else can."

"I beg your pardon?"

"You walk in, and you know what once happened there. Remember what you said at Shirley Plantation? About feeling a discontented Aunt Pratt?"

"If memory serves, you don't believe in my intuition. And in case you've forgotten, neither do I."

"No one knows what Jefferson intended with the Dome Room, but you might feel something once you're there."

"And if I don't?"

"I suppose you're free to go, if you'd like, but you're welcome to stay and pitch the project with me. Your talent with furniture qualifies you on its own."

"How much time do we have?"

"Prelim presentations are Monday, but if we make the cut to the final two, we'll have four weeks to—"

"Monday? As in four days from now?"

"Is that a problem?"

"We'll never make it, Scott, that's—"

"We'll make it. We don't waste time when we're together."

"Tell me honestly. What are our chances?"

"The University of Virginia has a deadlock on space number one, but we've got a legitimate shot at the second. And I never said I didn't believe in your eerie capability."

"You never said you did."

True, he hadn't.

Images of a fifteen-year-old crime scene flashed through his mind. Dark red blood had spilled over the walnut floor, seeping under the floral bed skirt. Her face—void of any bruises, for a change—vacant. Her glassy eyes, once warm and caring, testified an apparent truth— Ellie Sue Sheridan was no more.

And Molly would see it, too, if she entered the gate at Honey Hill.

*　　*　　*

She'd eaten too much, and now she was paying for it. Molly rinsed her plate and stowed it in the dishwasher. A leave of absence from Vaughan Appraisals, trekking out to the east coast with her ex-husband to submit a plan to the Board of Directors at Monticello… Couple that combination of life-stunning events with eating Star's entire platter of roast beef, and it was no wonder she felt queasy.

She knew, without eating much more than a few mouthfuls in days, ingesting rich food in abundance with Scott Sheridan on the brain was dumb, stupid, and idiotic.

As was following him on yet another patriotic discovery. She poured half a glass of merlot into the sink, cringing at its scent. *Never again.* This would be her last.

Last of gorging on oh-so-good food that was already clinging to her thighs. Last *pro bono* project of historical significance. Last love affair with Scott Sheridan.

But, damn it, it was going to happen. Her future unfolded before her like a road of yellow brick, and, without a thought, she was going to follow. Unlike its proverbial counterpart, however, it would lead her far from home.

*   *   *

"Hey, it's Sheridan." Scott paged through the paperback he'd purchased for Molly, holding the phone to his ear with his shoulder. "Thought you'd like to know your competition just got a little stiffer."

"You're always stiff, Dr. Sheridan." Dr. Stacie Wilkinson, professor of American History at the University of Virginia, yawned. "Have you any idea what time it is?"

Scott glanced at the clock. "Eleven o'clock on the east coast."

"Eleven-thirty."

"Come on, live a little."

"Your most annoying attribute is your late-night activity."

"I've got a list of references that say my 'late-night activity' ranks right up there with chocolate mousse."

"And involves it occasionally, if memory serves. What can I do for you, Sheridan? And make it quick. I'm not alone."

"Oh, so you *are* living a little without me. Good for you."

"What part of 'quick' don't you understand?"

"You know 'quick' isn't quite my style." He grinned.

"I'm hanging up."

"I bagged a furniture expert."

"What? How? No one's available. No one good anyway, who's willing to split the grant. Kingsley's at Carter's Grove, Hankins is at Stratford—"

"I'm not talking about an academic. I've got a real, hands-on furniture expert, and I'm gloating."

"You won't be when the board of directors turns a nose up at your layman."

"That's where you're wrong, Wilkinson. She's not a man at all. She's the daughter of two high-profile historians investigating hauntings at Blarney Castle in Ireland. And rumor has it she has a sixth sense of her own."

Silence hummed through the phone.

"Did you hear me?"

"Your ex-wife," Wilkinson finally said.

"That's right."

"Well, that's just terrific."

"Rattled, are we?"

"I'm not the one sleeping alone. You'll be distracted with the one who got away, or her ghost stories, and I'll sweep in to steal the deal. I should thank you really."

"Well, get on with it. I don't have all night."

"I don't have time for this."

"Good night, Wilkinson." He terminated the call.

CHAPTER 4

"Sweet Mother of God." Molly threw the plum-colored hood off her head and pressed her hands to her sweating temples. "For the thousandth time, I don't believe in psychic massage."

Dusky Loveday smiled from her cross-legged position on Molly's foyer floor. "This isn't a question of what you believe, but of what your mind directs your body to do. A little cool for shorts, isn't it?"

"Not when I'm running."

"And how was your jog this morning?"

"Peaceful, until I found you meditating in my foyer."

"Honey, this place is so packed with furniture, the foyer's the only place to connect my root center to the core of the earth without feeling crowded."

"And when Brandy said 'six,' she didn't specify 'in the morning.'"

Dusky swished her ample body to her feet and straightened the turquoise babushka that hid her wiry curls. "If you don't want visitors, you shouldn't leave your door unlocked. Hurry. I have to be to work in half an hour."

To Do List: Educate family about proper hours to visit. Molly followed the pull at her elbow, and before she knew it, she was sprawled on the foldaway massage table erected in the front room, sweating from head to toe from her early morning exercise. "Really, I don't think—"

"Relax, and let's get you balanced."

"I don't need balancing. I need a sane family and a shower."

35

"Girl, you're about as crooked as they come. Look at you. Your shoulders are out of line with your feet, and if you can't lie in a straight line, no way are you balanced."

"I just ran two miles, so give me a break."

Dusky hummed a few notes and pulled a small, wooden box from the folds of her teal linen skirt. From the box she extracted a crystal on a chain, which she held above Molly's head. Slowly, it began to move of its own volition. Back and forth, back and forth. Gradually, the minute movement spun into a wide, clockwise circle. "Well, well. Your connection with the divine is right on."

"I told you. I don't—"

Dusky's strong but gentle hands prohibited Molly from springing from the table. "Don't move, child. Six other centers need checking." She hovered the crystal above six other points along Molly's body line, interjecting an occasional "Mmm-hmm," and finally pocketed the crystal.

"Star's right about your core." She pressed her hands to Molly's stomach, and shifted her eyes around the room. "Ooh, and it's a powerful blue, encrusting your uterus. Something interrupted your plans for a family."

Damn America Windows. And she didn't need a psychic to remind her she was nearing thirty with no prospects for marriage. She had Aunt Star and a cocky ex-husband for that.

Dusky's thumbs kneaded her moist skin through the sweatshirt. "Imagine a gurgling stream, rushing through your body from head to toe. The water is fresh and pure enough to drink, and it's splashing against your uterine walls, dislodging this calcified blue as it flows."

Molly nodded, but the image did little more than intensify an urge to pee.

"It's the water of forgiveness, child, and you have a lot of forgiving to do before you take this eastward journey."

She snapped her eyes open. She hadn't told a soul about Scott's proposition, or her acceptance. "How did you—"

"Mirrors can be your best friend, if you stop judging what you see and accept it for what it is. You'll encounter many reflections along the way, and this blue will build, unless you allow the stream to wash it away. You must, lest it corrode your path of destiny."

"Am I interrupting something?" Scott's voice filtered in with the morning breeze.

Molly scrambled off the table to see her ex-husband peeking in the open front door. "Scottie."

"Hey, cupcake." He stepped into her foyer, wearing camel-colored corduroys and a long-sleeved denim shirt he hadn't bothered to tuck in over a crisp, white t-shirt. "Came to help you pack."

"Scott, this is my Aunt Dusky. She's here, um, well—"

"—for your rubdown. Of course." Scott smiled and extended a hand. "Good to meet you."

Dusky shook his hand and held it a moment longer than necessary. "Well, well. If it isn't Mr. Blue." She drummed her fingertips against her hips and stared at him, tapping her bare feet against the fir planks. "Interesting. Give us a minute, Molly?"

*　　*　　*

Scott hid a smile. *Endearing.* Molly had fans who wanted to protect her.

She chewed her succulent lower lip in arbitration, trading looks between him and Dusky.

"Go on, Miss Molly," he said. "I'll be all right."

"I'll just be a minute," she whispered on her way through the foyer. "I promise."

"By the way"—he brushed his index finger against her chin and then trailed it along the hollow of a cheek—"good morning."

Her lips parted as if she were going to say something, but she only shook her head and turned toward the stairs. She climbed steadily at a slow pace, every muscle in her pretty legs flexing. Graceful posture. He should have guessed years ago she was a dancer.

When walls obstructed his watching her any further, he turned to her visitor and pulled at his collar, feeling a surge of heat beneath his shirt. "What can I do for—"

"I'm more concerned with what I can do for Molly." Dusky folded her arms over her chest. "You've got issues I don't have time to describe, and you know what they are. This history with your folks, your mama and that gun."

An unsettling chill darted up Scott's spine, and his mouth suddenly tasted like cotton. It was bad enough he had to ponder the horrific event during sleep, but to confront it in waking hours … "Beg your pardon?"

"I don't give a diddly squat if you blame yourself."

"I don't know what you're—"

"But I do care about our tiny ballerina. Your strong hands are wrapped around her heart, and if you don't let go, you'll be no better than the pugilist your mama married."

He managed to summons his voice. "So you've done your research. Nice job. And tedious, too. Not much is public record."

"Honey, I don't dig into paperwork. I just read what I see." Dusky turned to her massage table and began to break it down. "And you're red. All of you. Piping hot passion, rage the color of fire. But fear so far beyond the boiling point I'm surprised you haven't burst."

"I don't believe in visions."

"I'm not telling you what to believe. I'm telling you what I see. Because I don't believe in repeating history."

"Neither do I."

"Well, that's something." Dusky banged the last table leg into its pocket and snapped it shut. She carried it like a briefcase toward the door.

"I know I broke her heart." He stuffed his hands into his pockets, fingered the antique ring he'd pinned there, and gave an abbreviated nod. "You're not the only one who sees things."

"Good bye, Mr. Blue."

"Let me get that for you." He took the table from her grasp and led her out the door.

Upon her squeezing his elbow, he turned to face her on the porch. A hand, tanned and leathery, reached out to press to his heart. "She might do you some good, too, you know," she whispered. "You're worried about what she might see when she sees the real you. Maybe you should worry about what might happen if you never give her the chance."

A tingling sensation numbed in his chest beneath her hand, and Scott stepped back. "Good meeting you, ma'am."

She dipped her head in a gracious nod and took the table from his grasp. "Take care of our girl."

"I wish I could." The instant he'd seen Molly on that dance floor, bending in ways no woman ought to be able to, every ounce of passion he carried for her had returned in a rush, settling in a vacant part of his heart.

But Dusky was right. With it came feelings of anger, hurt, and fear. Fear that Molly might someday learn the truth, simply by setting foot inside the mansion on Honey Hill.

The sound of rushing water echoed in the old Victorian's walls, and Scott stepped back inside, into the house Molly had told him about years ago, the house they'd daydreamed about owning together. A far cry from Virginia, it had seemed a welcome distraction from the ties binding him.

He yawned and stretched his stiff arms and legs, having endured a rough night. The same nightmares that had haunted him the day he'd buried his mother had stolen his peace last night—and, unfortunately, several other recent nights, too.

He'd never thought his mother capable of taking her own life. She hadn't left a note, but Scott knew—they all knew—she'd done it because she couldn't dodge another punch.

It wasn't easy sharing the name of a man who'd repeatedly beaten a lady into submission, but he hadn't chosen his own name, any more than he'd chosen his father.

Nothing would change *that* page in his family's history book. Ripping it out and burying it in a sealed court file hadn't stopped Dusky from knowing the truth. Perhaps it was only a matter of time before Molly knew it as well. Bringing his ex-wife back to Virginia was a risky move, but he couldn't allow an ancient mistake to interfere with what might solidify his career. He'd simply have to be careful—and keep her worlds away from Honey Hill.

The scents of Molly's home—old wood and antique furnishings—comforted him. A sanctuary from the discord of his past, Molly represented opportunity. Now, with Monticello on the horizon, and always. Serenity was there for the taking, just as California had been in the mid-1800s. Manifest Destiny.

He walked to the kitchen, entertained by the memory of Molly submersed in a random hotel tub, bubbles floating all around her wet body, mountains of hair piled atop her head.

He'd served her a continental breakfast in the tub once before, and that's what he'd do today, provided he could find his way around her kitchen. He opened the refrigerator and frowned. Lemon juice, rubbery celery, bottled water, a pint of skim milk, and half a stick of no-fat margarine. The freezer offered no better: one pound of ground turkey, a bag of sugar snap peas, one can of orange juice concentrate, and a twist-tied bag of large green grapes.

He traversed the kitchen, opening cupboards along the way. For someone who didn't stock groceries, she sure had a plethora of service pieces. *Come on, Molly, not even a can of corned beef hash?*

On the far side of the room stood a tall cabinet, deep brown rubbed through barn red, with an ornately carved pediment and curtained glass doors. *A pantry maybe?* He squeaked a door open to find a package of rice cakes, molding dried apricots, and unsalted microwave popcorn. This woman needed a rack of lamb in the worst of ways.

Just before he closed the pantry door, he spotted a dusty blender on the bottom shelf. "Hmm."

Minutes later, with two glasses of grape-orange smoothie in his grasp and her paperback book tucked into his back pocket, he nudged the bathroom door open to find her soaking in a white porcelain slipper tub, complete with brass footings and filled with iridescent bubbles. "Knock, knock."

With her pretty mouth open a fraction of an inch, she whipped her head toward him. "What are you—"

"Before you say anything, let me remind you, you're completely hidden with suds. And even if you weren't, I've done far more than look at you." He placed a smoothie in her hand and gave his head a shake, clucking his tongue. "Beautiful."

"I'm a mess."

"I meant the tub—"

"Kick me while I'm down."

"But I happen to like you when you're a mess." He sat on the black-and-white hexagonal tile floor, next to her rolled-up, discarded jogging shorts, and lifted his glass. "Here's to Molly in the morning."

"Scott." She shot him a warning glance.

"And, hey, have you ever heard of eating?"

"Eating?" Her cheeks flushed. "What did Dusky say to you?"

"Just the average 'take care of our gal or you'll be sorry.'"

"That's all?"

"It was enough."

She sipped her drink, leaving orange froth on her upper lip. She licked, but missed it.

"Here, let me." He brushed his thumb against her lip, and her smooth texture piqued a sweltering urge deep in his belly. Her gaze, smoldering like amber candles, practically dared him.

Kiss her. She wants it.

*   *   *

With every ounce of self-control she could muster, she refrained from wrapping her tongue around his thumb. Breathing suddenly became difficult. God, he was so ideal, physically speaking, and his intelligence could challenge her for decades on end. Her heart sank, mourning once again for their wasted love affair, and a familiar feeling

ANCIENT HISTORY

of emptiness encompassed her. She pulled away.

He cleared his throat. "If you hurry, we can grab breakfast."

Ugh. More food. "I don't have time for breakfast. If I'm going to take off an undetermined amount of time with two hours' notice, I should at least arrive before the boss and clear my desk."

"He'll miss you."

"Unlike some people, he actually needs me."

"Of course he does. You're very talented."

A far cry from "I'll always need you, too, Molly," but what did she expect? Of course he wasn't going to say something endearing. He was her ex-husband. Operative syllable being *ex.*

He clinked his glass against hers, sipped, and placed his drink atop the vanity. "Although without you, I'd miss our stunning conversations."

"We don't have conversations, Dr. Sheridan. We just...do...things."

"Hey, let's be fair, Miss Molly." He took the glass from her hand and set it aside. "When we're together, we both combust. You felt it yesterday, just like I did."

She nodded. "Sure, I felt it. But I'm entitled. I'm not the one with the divorce lawyer."

"I'm sorry about that, but—"

"You should be. I left my career behind to follow you on that book-signing excursion, and I thought I was bringing home a husband. Little did I know I'd be unloading him instead, for the sake of a buried journal at Tuckahoe Plantation."

"It turned out to be a hoax. No one's sorrier than I am."

"You're sorry for that damn journal." Amid uncontrollable rage and splashing water, she rose and glared at him.

"That and other things." He was staring, but not into her eyes.

In a split second, she remembered she'd been bathing before he'd riled her, and now she stood nude before him, bubbles tickling along her body. *Yikes.* She held one arm over her breasts and crossed her legs.

"See how quickly you crawl under my skin?" She yanked at her towel, but it refused to slip free from the bar. "How many other women forget they're naked in your company?" The towel gathered at the corner of the bar, bunched too thick to fall free.

"Like I said"—with one quick motion, he freed the towel, tossed it over her shoulders, and lifted her from the tub—"you don't mesh with simple ergonomic items." He held her close, the musky scent of his

41

aftershave flirting with her libido. "Charming."

"I hate you."

He blinked down at her and rubbed the towel against her wet skin in brisk strokes. His mouth parted an inch from hers, his ever-so-soft tongue flicking against his lower lip, while his gaze traveled to the hair shoved into a ponytail atop her head.

His glance flitted to her eyes, but quickly returned to her hair. "I have to," he whispered, unwinding the hair tie. Whenever he'd let her hair down in the past, he'd done so with painstaking care and patience, rubbing her scalp, twirling her curls around his fingers. This instance was no different. He leaned in close, brushing his cheek against hers and planting a kiss on her ear. "Can I wash it?"

"No."

"You can hate me all you want." His voice was as gruff and seductive as it had been the first night they'd made love. "Doesn't change the fire between us."

"I don't hate you. I don't hate anyone. Bad karma in hate."

He lifted her chin with a finger, and she blinked into his emerald gaze, greener and brighter with passion. There she went again, falling into those shamrocks as if she'd plunged off a cliff.

"Oh, no."

"Oh, yes." He scrunched her hair.

"You don't want this, Scottie."

He twirled her hair between his fingers, every breath bringing their mouths a millimeter closer. "I know what I want."

"Until the moment you get it." A door slammed on the level below, jolting each of them and leaving Molly's towel in a pool at her ankles.

"Just Gracie." He fingered a curl and pressed her wet body against the plaster, bath water bleeding through his shirt.

"Molly!" came a shrill scream from the staircase.

"Not Gracie." Molly tensed and reached for another towel. *To Do List: Practice locking the front door.* "My cousin."

Brandywine's feet scampered up the stairs. "I know you're here because your car's out front. Molly?"

He covered her body with his, encapsulating her against the wall, just in time to conceal her nudeness from Brandywine.

Eyes like saucers, her cousin turned her back to the couple. "Interrupting, am I?"

"Genius, Brandy." She pulled the towel up and around her torso with Scott's help. "Don't people knock anymore?"

"Hey, we used to share a bedroom. If you suddenly expect privacy, you need to lock your door." Brandy tapped her feet and folded her arms over her chest. "How many times do I have to teach you the trick? Turn the key, lift up on the knob, twist."

Molly secured the towel and shoved hair from her eyes. "Scott, this is my cousin."

"At last, a formal introduction." Brandywine spun around and flashed her brightest smile. "Brandywine Townsend."

"Interesting name." Scott draped Molly's hair across her shoulder as she moved away.

*   *   *

Hours later, with a belly full of biscuits and gravy from Fred's Diner on Center Street, Scott stacked crates of text books on Molly's front porch. He'd used her plentiful library as an excuse for them to drive to Charlottesville, in lieu of catching a flight. They could plan their presentation on the way, but time in the car would be good for them. They'd be alone on the road—just as they had been five years ago.

Bells of a nearby church tolled nine. He put his fists on his hips and breathed the heavy, humid air, taking in the sight of Park Avenue in the morning. Not a soul passed without waving, and a constant breeze—Molly had called it a "lake effect"—softened the sticky dampness of the day.

The house was as charming as any he'd lived in, complete with a private balcony overlooking the front garden off the master bedroom. Perhaps someday they'd enjoy a sunrise on that veranda, after a long night of lovemaking. A private oasis, away from the children they'd someday have, they'd share a glass of wine, read together up there, and wave to the mailman everyone knew.

Such a captivating town. And it could have been his home, had he managed to resist using as his excuse to leave Wilkinson and the rumored find at Tuckahoe five years ago. Parker's Landing reminded him of the east coast: old buildings and proud citizens. And the town's famous Gray's Lake was a far cry from the Rappahannock River and the salty sea air of his childhood home, but he'd heard the fishing was good. And Fred's biscuits and gravy was nothing to sneeze at either. He patted his stomach with a satisfied smile.

Perhaps his contentment had nothing to do with food; after all, how could a northern greasy spoon compete with Southern fare? But maybe his satisfaction was the direct result of his proximity to Molly.

If that were the case, he'd better get over it. And fast. She'd forever chase a path paved by some ridiculous source of divinity, and he... Well, as much as he hated to admit it, he'd always have another research project, another historical find commanding his attention in Virginia. And it was imperative he keep Molly a safe distance from the house there in which his life had changed forever. Should she ever step into his mother's boudoir, she'd know the whole, ugly truth—and the role he'd played in it.

She pulled into the red-brick drive, her tired smile promising the pot of gold at the end of the rainbow.

"How'd it go?" Scott asked, rolling his sleeves.

"I'm ready to finish packing." She propped her sunglasses on the top of her head, framing her signature bun, and exited the car. "Did you find that hatbox yet?"

"No, but, Lord, I'd love to see you pounding away on that dance floor. I found tap shoes by the dozens up there."

She meandered up the walk, studying her home, and drew in a long, deep breath. "I'm going to miss it."

"I told Gracie we'd write." He grinned, but she didn't crack a smile. "Easy, Miss Molly. It's just a quick jaunt out to Virginia. Not forever."

"I'm perfectly well aware of that, Dr. Sheridan."

Sharp words, and they sliced through his heart. "Molly, I need you." Her dark glance darted to his. Powerful.

"You have a talent I can't begin to understand, and you're my ace in the hole, but if this trip—"

"I'm not promising any miracles, but I'm game, Scott. I can take it, if you can."

"Absolutely."

"On one condition—no hotels. We drive straight through to Charlottesville."

"And once we get there?"

"We'll figure it out."

He'd rather figure her in.

"And no cards." She shaded her eyes from the sun, looking up at him. "No draws off the deck this time."

He traced the white gold scrolls on the ring in his pocket. "Whatever you say, cupcake."

"And no more with the 'cupcake.' I have a name."

"I know your name."

"My entire name?"

"Give me a minute." A smile crept onto his face. "It'll come to me."

With a furrowed brow, she climbed the porch stairs. Lord, he could watch her move for decades on end. Observing that body on a dance floor touched him in places he'd forgotten he had.

She turned to him with a curt stop, one toe digging into the slatted porch floor, knee slightly bent. "What was Martha Jefferson's middle name?"

"Wife or daughter?"

"Wife."

"She was known as Martha Wayles Skelton Jefferson, but those were most likely surnames."

"And she married Tom when?"

"New Year's Day, 1772, at the Forest Plantation."

"Quite a memory of the first lady."

"Actually, she died nineteen years before Jefferson served as president. If you want to get technical, his first lady was—"

"Sally Hemings?" Her pretty mouth drew into a kissable pucker, and her eyes glimmered in challenge.

He inched closer to her, taking her soft hand, never losing the contact of her intriguing stare. "His daughter Martha, whom he called Patsy, served as first lady during a brief stay in the White House."

"First term or second?"

"First. Winter, 1802. Gave birth to the first child ever born there."

"Named?"

"For James Madison."

"And we were married on?"

"April thirteenth."

Her lashes flickered, and her body became a warm, pliable mass in his arms. "You remember," she whispered, her lips brushing against his.

"Of course—"

"I never dreamed in a million years you'd—"

"—it's Thomas Jefferson's birthday."

In a quick motion, she slipped from his arms and, after banging her slim hip against the door to open it, disappeared behind it.

"A day made even more special," he muttered, although she'd skipped halfway up the stairs and couldn't possibly hear, "because of you. The way I felt about you."

CHAPTER 5

"Tired?" Amid a flash of lightning, Scott glanced to the passenger seat, where Molly hugged her knees. Her feet threatened to creep across the car's center console onto his lap at any moment, and the seat belt cradled her face.

"Mmm-hmm." The sound, both satisfied and seductive, escaped from her lips, as if she were well on her way to dreamland. She looked as cozy as she had years ago, when he'd found her sleeping in a front-porch rocker at a charming bed and breakfast in Jefferson's country. That night, she'd been wearing the same type of pants she wore today. Now he knew she was a dancer, it made more sense that she'd called them "jazz pants."

Scott placed a steady hand at an opportune location where her thigh met her hip. Firm. He pictured her on Amelia's dance floor, her leg high on a *barre*, graceful and curvaceous. "I'll find a hotel."

"We agreed no hotels." As cutting as she probably meant her words to be, they flowed from her lips like honey off a spoon.

"I've got another thirty miles in me, tops. Are you ready to take over?"

"Mmm-hmm."

Again, he glanced in her direction, memories of the tender twenty-three days she'd been his wife—not to mention the preceding six he'd spent wooing her—coursing through his veins, rushing, like a first kiss. "We're stopping for the night."

"I can drive."

No, she couldn't. He'd been touching her for at least sixty seconds, and she'd yet to push his hand away. "You're too tired to drive."

"Mmm-hmm."

He felt the corner of his mouth peak in triumph. Her breathing evened into a metronomic rhythm, keeping time with the windshield wipers. During his childhood, rain had relaxed him, evoking images of a sleepy fishing shack along the Rappahannock River. Ever since he'd served Molly with divorce papers during a thunderstorm, however, he'd felt uneasy in the rain.

His mother used to say rain was the angels' way of washing sin away, and while that rationale had comforted him during storms at age seven, he'd learned the truth the moment he'd found his mother with that revolver. Ellie Sue Sheridan didn't know a thing about negating sin. Rain equaled *America Windows* equaled Molly. Period. Nothing could erase all he'd done to crush his ex-wife's spirit, least of all rain and the memory of long-gone Mama.

The highway lights rolled over Molly's exhausted figure, illuminating her beauty. Leaving her to pursue something as historically insubstantial as a false find had been insane. He knew now that Wilkinson had practically dared him, and he'd fallen into her trap. At the time, Wilkinson's request for his expertise had been a welcome diversion, an option to telling Molly the truth about his mother. But now, it was nothing more than a dirty trick—and not just on Wilkinson's part.

On the right hand side of the interstate, a billboard boasted accommodations: Courtyard Hotel, Super 8, next exit. To hell with what he'd promised. He needed to wrap Molly in his arms, to wake up with her, to feel as special as she'd made him feel all those years ago. Clothed or otherwise.

He steered the car onto the next ramp. The lights of several hotel signs beckoned in the distance, but before he reached any of them, a flickering neon arrow caught his attention—Doomie Inn. By the hour.

"Oh, I have to see this." He drove onto a dirt path, overhung by thick trees. It led to a well-kept clapboard farmhouse with a wide dormer peeking out from the steep pitch of the roof. Scattered throughout the property were eight tiny cottages, sided with white slats and isolated amid the quaint, wooded property.

"Perfect."

Molly shifted in her sleep, but even his exit—the influx of wet wind, the slamming of the car door—did nothing to rouse her from much needed rest. He hurried through the rain to the door.

A handwritten *Ring the bell for assistance* note prompted him to do just that.

After a few moments, a woman's voice sounded—gravelly, smoky, and pure Kentucky—through the intercom. "How can I help?"

"One room please."

"For how long?"

"The night."

"Come in."

A buzzer zapped, and he opened the door. The scent of broasted chicken and—he sniffed—something buttery accosted him. He glanced around the room. Light from a muted television set flickered over a matronly, navy blue couch. Molly would have called it a sofa. Silence, save the buzz emanating from the TV, crawled from every nook and cranny of the lazy home.

A middle-aged woman wearing an orange terrycloth robe as dreary as her face, peeled herself up from the couch. "Right with you."

"Sorry to wake you," Scott said.

She groaned, slumped across the worn, beige carpeting to a round, aluminum table, and waved a hand at one of the chairs. "Have a seat."

Interesting. No scent of whiskey on her breath. He would have bet—

"Paying in cash?"

"Do you take credit cards?"

"No."

"Then cash it is."

"Whole night, you said?"

"That's right."

"Number five's clean. Forty-three dollars for a key. Leave the key in the room when you're done."

"We'll be out early." Scott tented a crisp fifty on the table. The tossed key clanked against the surface.

"You need change, or are you in a hurry? I got to go up to the safe to get it."

"Why should I be the only one getting lucky? Keep it."

The innkeeper shoved the bill into her robe pocket, shuffled to the sofa, and spilled back into it.

"Have a nice night," Scott said, exiting into the brutal weather. He drove around to cottage number five and carried in their duffel bags.

From his post in the pouring rain, leaning into the car, Scott unfastened his ex-wife's seat belt and shook her with a gentle hand. "Molly, wake up. We're here."

She sighed, not budging.

"Honey, we're home."

His words weren't enough to wake her, but the crack of thunder sent her springing upward in her seat. Her mysterious brown eyes opened, and she blinked to take in her surroundings. "Wh—where? What?"

"We're in Lexington."

"Virginia?"

He chuckled. "No, cupcake. Lexington, Kentucky."

"You said—"

"To hell with what I said, I'm getting drenched out here. Are you coming, or are you sleeping in the car?"

A delicate finger swept from one corner of her eye to the other. "I'll—"

Another crash of thunder.

He pulled her out of the car and tossed her over his shoulder.

"Put me down, professor." She squirmed in his embrace, feet kicking, arms flailing.

"You're slippery when wet. I'll drop you if you don't—"

No sooner said, she slid off his shoulder. He scrambled to catch her, and when she slipped through his hands again, he lunged to break her fall.

Waters of a cool and certainly dirty puddle seeped through his jeans and splashed against his back as gravel dug into the heels of his hands. But something comfortable, warm, and lilac-scented lay against his chest, pressed between his legs. When he gained his bearings, he registered that comfortable being as Molly—and she was almost as wet as he.

"Oh!" She glared at him, pulled herself to her feet and kicked water at him. "What are you—fifteen?"

"Hey, I think I took the brunt of that battle." He climbed out of the puddle and shook water from his hair.

"You deserve everything you—" The rage in her eyes turned to shock, the neon sign flashing Doomie, Doomie, Doomie reflecting off her irises. "Tell me I'm still asleep. Tell me you didn't bring me to a seedy, rank motel called the Do Me Inn."

"You want me to lie to you?" He gripped her under the elbow and began to guide her toward the cottage.

"I'm soaking wet."

"I guess we'll both have to slip into something more comfortable."

"Shut up."

"It's clean, Molly. Seventies décor, with a baby blue toilet. And festive." He shoved open the door to reveal knotty pine walls, strings of Christmas lights hanging around the perimeter of the room, and—

"Mirrors on the ceiling? Are you insane?" She whacked him on the chest with a stinging slap. "I'm not staying here."

"I don't know where else you're going to go."

She offered her hand, palm up. "Give me the keys."

"Take them." He planted his fists on his hips, his bulk filling the doorway.

"Where are they?"

"If you can find them, they're all yours."

"I hate you."

*   *   *

Molly didn't sift through the passion that had exploded in the room over the decades, though plenty steamed from every nook and cranny. She was too busy staring at her marvelous ex-husband, pouting like a little boy.

His already-tired eyes closed a fraction and he slipped a hand into his pocket. The keys jingled into view, and he turned toward the door. "Keep the room. I'll sleep in the car."

"Don't be ridiculous." She caught his elbow.

"You say it a lot, for someone who insists she doesn't hate anyone."

"You dropped me in a mud puddle, half-asleep, for crying out loud. What did you expect?"

"After watching you on that dance floor, I expected at least one of us might land on our feet."

"I might have, if I'd had any warning, but you—"

"Imagine my surprise to see you there." His subdued voice matched the smolder in his eyes. "You made love out of that music, you know that? Passion flowing from your heart straight out the tips of your toes."

"Do you always say things you don't mean to get what you want?"

"Why do you assume I don't mean what I say?"

She turned toward a small, scarred end table and caught sight of her reflection in a burnished, rectangular mirror hanging above an abused sofa. Her hair sprang out from an oversized claw clip like a volcano erupting, and mascara dripped in a tiny rivulet at the corner of her left eye. "The room is fine." *Sultry, sexy.* She smeared the mascara into a smudge. "Not as in 'fine furnishings,' or 'fine china'—obviously—but satisfactory. You don't have to sleep in the car."

He dropped the keys back into his pocket. "Why don't you grab a hot shower? I'll get out of these wet clothes and troll for some snacks."

"It's too late to eat."

"We didn't have much of a dinner."

"Yeah, well, I ate too much yesterday."

"You sure?"

The thought of Star's overflowing platter of roast beef threatened to turn her stomach. And she did *not* look too thin. "Yes."

"Not just about the snack."

She glanced around the room. Double bed, adequate quarters. "Who am I to resist a vintage blue commode?"

"Ah, so you trust me?" Without awaiting her response, he bolted the door and zapped her with a cool, emerald stare.

A chill swept over her flesh as she met his gaze, raising goose bumps on her arms and making party hats of her nipples. Was it the temperature of the room or the company that had affected her so? His tongue appeared for a split second on his bottom lip. *Such talent in that moist muscle.* She remembered it all too well.

"I trust you," she said too softly, rubbing her upper arms with brisk strokes. *Trust, ha.* She trusted he could have her on her back in seconds flat, if he so desired.

He pulled a damp paperback book from his duffel bag, tossed it onto the bed, and brushed past her stimulated body. "Cold?"

"No."

"There's one way to warm you up." A devilish grin appeared in his lips.

"I'd rather freeze."

"I was talking about a hot shower."

"Oh."

"You want it first, or—"

"Yes, if you don't mind."

"Be my guest." He shrugged off his water-splotched sweatshirt, grey with a navy W overlapping an L to look like a trident: Washington and Lee University. The thin, damp t-shirt beneath, which bore the same logo, did little to hide his muscled chest.

Although she tried not to think about it, glimpses of his defined

51

body flashed through her mind—an abdomen that looked as if it had been carved in stone, broad shoulders with a raised scar on the rear of the right one. Thank goodness she had an excuse to hightail it away from the bed, or she'd rip off his shirt. And she knew where that would lead—to a rumbling mass under the covers.

Halfway to the bathroom, she looked over her shoulder to see Scott stepping out of his jeans. She snapped her gaze away, slipped into the bathroom, and leaned against the door.

She slowly released a breath—*oh, my*—and stripped off her wet, muddy clothing. After rewrapping her hair into a twist and securing it with a claw clip, she stepped into the tub.

Pull it together, Molly. A long few weeks ahead of you.

And not off to a great start either, considering she couldn't shake the desire to dart back to the bed and couldn't work the shower.

She turned the faucet handle in a continuous circle amid a chilly, though energetic, stream, which never got warmer. "Come on, give me some hot water." Drops of icy water ricocheted off the baby blue tub surround, and only when the water obviously would not warm up did she step under it. With one arm shielding her body from the cold spray, she yanked the plastic shower curtain closed. "Thanks for nothing, Gracie."

"Gracie's a long way from home, isn't she?"

She jumped. "Scottie!"

Not more than his hand invaded her shower. He twisted the knob. "Getting warmer?"

"How did you do that?"

"Rocket science. This here, cupcake, is a valve." He patted the handle with his index. "Turn it to the left, and it lessens the cold water supply."

"You think I didn't try that?"

"Show me."

"Show you what?"

Palm up, he wiggled his fingers. "Give me your hand."

Hesitantly, she placed her hand in his, and he pressed it against the shower handle, his fingers massaging hers.

"This shower's older than you are. Needs a little finesse, that's all. Get a feel for it. Don't spin the handle. Wait for it to catch. See?"

"I got it. Thanks."

"Need any more help in there? Washing your back, taking your hair down? Anything?"

She closed her eyes, warm at last, and imagined him imprisoning her against the blue tile, her legs locked around his waist, their wet bodies melded together. "No."

"If you change your mind—"

"I'll be quick." Minutes later, wrapped in a thin towel, she perched on the side of bed. When Scott disappeared behind the narrow bathroom door, she reached for her cell phone and dialed her cousin. "Brandy, tell me I can do this."

"So you're going to sleep with him, huh?"

"I meant, tell me I can do this *without* sleeping with him."

"Girlfriend, I don't know how, but if you find a way to resist that hunk of—"

"Brandy, I don't need you to remind me of his fine pectorals. What I need is a backbone here."

"Okay, fine, I'll lie to you—you can do it. But judging by what I interrupted in your bathroom this morning, I'd say it's more overdue than inevitable."

"That's not why I agreed to do this, you know. If getting laid was what I wanted, I could've done that back home." Molly rubbed at a callus on her big toe, a remnant from years *en pointe*. *To do list: Pedicure.* "Why are you so quiet all of a sudden?"

"You never date. How do you expect to get laid?"

"I *can* date. I choose not to."

"No need for explanations. Star wants to know how it's going with the blue in your aura."

"Dusky did her best."

"Good."

"More like frightening. Everything around me is blue, including the toilet at this motel, and—" She clamped her mouth shut, a vague memory of white gold and a sapphire settling upon her. "My ring."

"What?"

"Nothing. Suddenly I remembered that my wedding ring had a sapphire instead of a diamond."

"Cheap bastard. He's adorable, but he could use a lesson in—"

"No, it was an antique. Perfect for me. And blue."

"Popular color this week."

"Focus. Star sensed I had to flush out the blue and leave it in the past. Dusky said something blue impeded my having a family. We all assumed it was *America Windows*, but maybe it's my ring or something else altogether. So am I supposed to forget my marriage? Or my divorce?"

"How the hell should I know? My gift for sight ends with my pupils."

"Rub Chubs' belly for me. Good karma, good karma."

"Sure."

"God, what am I supposed to do?"

"I'm no god, but I'll tell you what I'd be doing: six-feet-two-inches of green-eyed gorgeous. Come on, Mol, do him. Do him for me and women everywhere."

Molly sighed heavily, rolling her eyes. "He isn't as ideal as he looks, you know."

"I've had a bit of experience in the ideal market lately."

"New guy? Pray tell."

"No, I don't want jinx it. So...did you eat today?"

"Yes."

"You swear?"

"I'm not anorexic. Just preoccupied."

"What did you have for dinner?"

"Dried apricots and vanilla yogurt."

"That isn't food. That's an enema."

"It's food. It's just—" Scott's hand on her shoulder silenced her. How much had he heard? She looked into the mirror on the ceiling, hesitant to look him in the eye.

Illuminated with the red and green Christmas lights strung about the walls, his reflection was stunning enough to draw her attention from Brandywine's ramblings about protein. She stared at a shoulders-down-to-his-boxers view of his bare back. Not quite tan, but then, it was early May, and he'd probably holed himself in his office, grading final exams. Fine with her; his olive-toned skin still tempted her like a creamy dessert.

And there it was—the scar on his shoulder. She fought the urge to touch it and focused on his disheveled hair, damp from either the rain or the shower. She could think of nothing but raking her fingers through it.

She blinked away from the mirrored ceiling and into his gaze. *Oh, no! Shouldn't have done that.* Butterflies rushed to parts of her she shouldn't want to acknowledge while he stood this close. "Hi."

He nodded, biting that beautiful lower lip. "Hi."

"Call you later." She closed her phone, drowning out her cousin's lecture. "Let me guess—can't work the shower?"

His fingers trailed from her shoulder to the upper portion of her back, caressing like soft waves. "Shower's fine. I'm done." He lifted her chin in a hand. "You okay?"

"Sure."

"Thanks for coming, if I never said it."

"You did."

He brushed his thumb against her cheek and turned to step into a fresh pair of jeans. "I'm going to find a Laundromat and get something to eat. What do you want?"

The view of Scott Sheridan, casually stuffing plaid boxer shorts into jeans with a lazy comfort, stunned her. And the place was so overloaded with mirrors, she couldn't look away without catching another tempting angle. What did she want, indeed. "You."

He snapped his head up, and she refrained from smacking herself. All right, so it was true. Did she have to be so blunt about it?

Within seconds, he'd kicked off his jeans, crawled onto the bed, and leaned over her. His lips parted into a playful grin.

She pressed her hands against his oh-so-hard chest, but her strength was no match for his determination. "You didn't let me finish," she whispered.

He worked the clip, freed her hair, and buried a hand in the tangled mass. "You always finish before me. It's one of the things I love about you." He kissed her, lowering her to her back.

He *loved* things about her? *Yikes.* And jeez, he worked fast, nudging a knee between her thighs.

"I meant that I—"

"I know what you meant." Amid a barely-there brush on her lips, his nose rubbed against hers. His mouth traveled like a hot mist over her neck, her shoulders. He pushed her towel aside. *Good riddance.*

His flesh melted against her body, and a searing need to feel all of him rushed through her veins. She tucked a toe into his boxers and, using her feet, tugged the underwear over his hips. All those dancing lessons were good for something.

The view on the ceiling took her breath away. His muscular rear end, a shade whiter than his back, was working its way between her thighs, which from this point of view didn't look too fat after all.

She fingered the scar on his shoulder, wrapped her legs around him, and registered the line of his hips in direct conjunction with hers.

He scrunched her mass of unruly ringlets, and swept it aside. His lips landed upon her mouth in a precise, sweet kiss, his tongue searching hers in a leisurely saunter. "Molly Catherine," he whispered against her lips.

A soft groan rumbled in her throat. "So you remember."

He dragged a few fingers along the contour of a breast, his thumb tracing circles around her nipple. "I could never forget."

Her every muscle tightened and she lifted her hips, grinding subtly, feeling him grow and harden against her.

"I want to look at you," he whispered, kissing a path from her mouth to her navel, his hands following the trail. On his haunches between her spread-eagle legs, he slipped a finger into her private confines and looked to the mirror on the ceiling. "Good Lord, look at you."

She arched against the mattress, his index finger stroking her into a slick frenzy, and gauging her reflection, she had to admit it: she did look good with his hands on her.

He repositioned himself at her side, his gaze blanketing her from top to toe, lingering. Another finger joined the mix below, and he shoved the thumb on his opposite hand into her mouth. "When you look like this, I want to fill you from both ends. At the same time."

Yes, fill me. Her lips puckered at the base of his thumb, and she sucked on it meticulously, focused on the pleasure surging between her legs.

He stroked her in a languid rhythm, alternating fingers, and, in response, she bit down on his thumb, humming out her pleasure. One finger swirled, the other dragged. Swirl and drag, swirl and drag, against a deep pocket inside her, conjuring pleasure from all corners of the world. Building and gathering energy like a gypsy spell about to break into a storm.

Thunder crashed outside, and lightning flashed through the windows like a strobe, brightening the mirror, illuminating the reflection on the ceiling.

Her cheeks went hollow with suction and her thighs tensed.

His tongue flattened against her clit and his lips closed around it.

"Ohhhh." The pleasure built and snowballed, and she watched all of it in the mirror on the ceiling: Scott's head in a subtle bob between her legs, his thumb twisting in her mouth, his fingers dragging against her insides, provoking her, leading her over the brink. She held her arch with discipline, desperately grasping the linens, and with her tongue, she forced his thumb out of her mouth. *Must breathe.*

"Oh, Scottie." When her orgasm broke, she sank against the

mattress, the shower of pleasure unrelenting, her breaths uneven and rapid.

He pulled his fingers from her body and crawled over her, pressing his erection to her hard, stimulated clit. "I've been thinking about that for years."

"Don't lie to me."

"Not lying." He lowered his mouth to hers in a soft, open-lipped kiss.

Buddha in Headstand. Good karma. She certainly deserved the love. But could she trust he'd remember the reciprocity that ought be involved in a love affair? They'd already played the one-sided-relationship gig. When the teeter didn't totter, the game had come to an abrupt and brutal end.

He whisked his hand under a pillow, and a square, gold foil package spun out from under it.

"Planned ahead, didn't you?" Should she be thankful or offended with his assumption?

With a shrug, he bit into the wrapping and shook the prophylactic into her hand. Her decision: to sheathe or not to sheathe—and thus, to do or not to do?

His deltoid muscles flexed, inviting her to run a hand over the topography of his back. Her gaze locked on the mirror above them, and after fixating on his scar, she took in every other detail. Black, disheveled hair, the clean scent of soap, the gruff feel of his whiskers at her cheek. Would this be the last hurrah she'd pondered back in Parker's Landing? Or was this the first event in a new ramshackle affair?

God help her—any god, of any religion since now was not the time to be particular—to do what was best. She couldn't recover from another failed relationship with her ex. Her aunt thought she was thin now, but five years ago—

Scott feathered her neck with kisses and again pressed his hips to her pelvis. The length of him—hard and ready—sent a tickling sensation directly to her g-spot, and an odd image entered her mind of blue stalactites melting to a serene pool.

She had no time to decipher the message. Not when she concentrated on his shaft rubbing her clit, his balls brushing against her opening. *Oh, yes.* Sex with this man was definitely the thing to do. Right or wrong...well, she'd figure that out later.

He whispered a seductive, "Miss Molly," the moment she stroked the condom over him, kneading his hard flesh with her thumb from tip to base.

Within seconds, he persuaded her lips to part with a sweep of his tongue. He gripped her ankle and slowly raised her leg, pinning her in a vertical split.

*   *   *

"Oh, Molly." Their reflection on the ceiling resembled something out of his hottest wet dream. His ex-wife nibbled her lip and stared into the mirror, too, watching as his cock disappeared, inch by inch, into the moist silkiness between her legs.

Once completely inside her, he allowed his gaze to roam to other reflections: her flat tummy, her perky breasts and bronze nipples, the spray of freckles across her nose, and the auburn curls atop her head. "You're so pretty."

She tensed. "Stop looking at me."

"I can't." He glanced back to the mirror. "You're incredible, cupcake." With steady gyrations, he continued to plunge into her, every drive home spurring magic. Sweet spot, right there judging by the way she groaned each time he hit it.

The view above amazed him, but suddenly, the reflection didn't rate compared to the real woman. He blinked down at her, realizing the truth of what he'd said. Not looking at her was not possible. And neither was not kissing her.

He lowered his lips to hers, curled in a provocative "O." The sealing of their mouths, sugary and passionate, fueled the fire between them, enticed him to seek every inch of her body, to find, to know.

Starting with the back of her neck.

With gentle force, he pressured her leg, still pinned in a split, across her body. He turned her over, twisting her on his cock. Once on her stomach, she lifted her hips to him, welcoming deep penetration. The soft triangle of hair at her apex tickled his balls, and her fingers followed suit, grazing against him, rubbing, tugging.

He swept her hair off her neck and deposited a wet kiss there, inhaling lilac from her tresses. Her hips bucked against him, matching his rhythm, and oh, what he wouldn't have given to see her swivel those hips on a dance floor. Or better yet, on a private stage.

The image wouldn't leave his mind; he gripped her waist with enough force to ensure he'd made an impression, but not so much to leave a mark.

He traced an imaginary line down her spine. "Come with me."

Not just here in bed. Not only to Monticello. But always.

Her hips rose to meet his every thrust, and their bodies fit together like puzzle pieces. Click.

"It's been this good since the first time," he whispered. "Do you remember?"

She breathed a sweet sigh. Of course she remembered.

He looked up to the mirror on the ceiling. The sight was enough to finish him off: his hands cupping a perfect rear-end, mounds of wild, red-brown hair bouncing against her arched back, his cock buried in a body he never dreamed he'd be inside again.

But something nagged at him from deep within his conscience. He wasn't screwing. And she wasn't a body. She was his ex-wife, and he couldn't justify finishing in their present—though unbelievable—position. He wanted to kiss her as he came—her mouth, her eyes, her neck—to hold her tight, and feel her shiver in his embrace.

CHAPTER 6

Sex like this took his mind on a dangerous journey. The things that had entered his thoughts… Lord, it was no small wonder that five years ago, he'd led her to an altar after six short days—before he'd learned of her uncanny ability with the history of old homes.

They breathed in unison, hearts clamoring against one another in the aftermath. He looked down into her eyes and brushed a curl from her forehead. Her legs remained locked around his waist, her bony hips nudging up toward his pelvis in one last, mystical compression.

"Oh, Miss Molly." Her breasts crushed against his chest when he leaned to her lips. "The things you do to me."

"Order a pizza," she whispered into his kiss. "I'm hungry."

He rolled her over, chuckling and positioning her on top. "Four cheese and spinach on a thick crust."

"That's right."

*   *   *

He remembered how she liked her pizza. First he'd remembered her middle name, and now this. It didn't mean anything. So he'd recalled a few details, so he'd given her the most thorough chain of orgasms she'd had in years. That certainly didn't equate to giving their relationship another go.

"I can do pizza." He closed his lips over her chin and gave her a playful nibble. "It's good to know you still eat. There's nothing left of you, you're so thin."

The stroke of his hand en route from her thigh to her hip and back again enticed relaxation. "I eat."

"When and what?"

"Pizza...and soon, I hope."

"Nothing like lounging with a pizza and my best girl on the couch."

"That one looks like a mass of broken springs. Oh, I never finished telling you. In 1976, the Jeffries family donated the Duncan Phyfe to the University of Virginia on two conditions. One: It was not to be altered in any way. Two: No one was to sit on it."

"Shush." He cradled her face and, smiling, drew her closer for another deep kiss.

"But the university reupholstered it in a lime green moiré taffeta, and—"

"Shh."

His lips encompassed hers and she shut up, unable to fight the smile coming on. So this was what happiness was like. Images of blue glass flashed through her mind—smiling children, dancing girls, books denoting higher learning. America. And with Scott Sheridan, the American dream seemed possible.

She rolled off him and reached for the phone book. But why, if he'd loved her, had he failed to incorporate her into *his* dream?

The question still danced on the tip of her tongue an hour and four slices of pizza later. With a floor plan of Monticello spread across the bed they'd recently defiled, and blue self-adhesive notes dotting the paper, she lay across his lap, wearing his discarded Washington and Lee t-shirt.

He combed through her hair with one hand, pausing only to turn the pages of the historical fiction he'd purchased for her back in Parker's Landing. With glasses perched on his nose, he read aloud, only occasionally interjecting factoids regarding the Jefferson-Hemings affair.

Molly knew that, while Scott admitted to Jefferson's knowing his slave in a conjugal manner—proven with DNA testing of the Hemings' descendants—he didn't believe Tom had loved Sally. Perhaps Jefferson had viewed her much in the same way Scott had seen Molly—as his natural born right—manifest destiny.

If the parallel were true, the professor probably hadn't loved her either.

She stared at her reflection on the ceiling, watched his hand work against her scalp as if he'd been lulling her to sleep this way every night for the past five years. But if he hadn't loved her, why had it felt so real? And why did it feel real now?

*   *   *

Scott awoke the next morning to a vague knocking, which sounded like a woodpecker hammering a distant tree. The song of mourning doves filtered through the closed window, and first light illuminated the pine paneled walls of the cottage.

He rolled over to envelope Molly in his arms, only to find her pillow empty. The bathroom door stood open, and none of the numerous mirrors in the place boasted her reflection. "Molly?"

"Yes." Her muffled answer sounded as if it were coming from just outside the window.

A quick peek showed no sign of her. "Where are you?"

"At the door. Let me in."

He glanced at the clock. *Not even six.* "Good Lord." He crawled from bed, nude, and opened the door to his sweating ex-wife, her hair piled in a haphazard ball atop her head and secured with a black hair tie.

"The key's stuck in the door." She shouldered past him.

He removed the key without so much as a jiggle. "Morning jog?"

"I needed it. I ate half a pizza yesterday. And not just any pizza, a large pizza with buttery crust and umpteen pounds of cheese."

"You worked those calories off before you ate them." He tossed the key atop his jeans, which she'd laid across a rickety chair to dry. Had she investigated the contents of his pockets? If she'd found the ten-of-hearts or her wedding ring pinned in the pocket, she'd ask about the items sooner or later. He'd better have an explanation ready and waiting.

"About last night..." She sat on the edge of the bed and untied her shoelaces.

"I think 'Wow' just about covers last night." He crept onto the mattress, hooked her under an arm, and pulled her back to bed. Their legs entwined when he leaned over her.

"I need a shower." She struggled to escape his hold.

He tightened his grip. "You're only going to sweat more."

"We should get going. We have to be on plantation grounds first thing Monday morning, and we've yet to set foot in a library."

"I don't need a library right now. I need you."

"We have to compare notes, enter the curator's office united."

62

"I'll show you united."

Her skin was cool and damp against his. There was something about the perspiration of a woman misting over his flesh that caused a percolating between his legs. He groaned, slid a hand under her sweatshirt, and cupped a breast, squashed in a jogging bra.

Her shoes hit the floor with a thud, which meant she'd shoved them off. *Good sign.* He briskly ran a hand along her ribs, from breast to hip. Why she assumed she needed to work off calories was beyond him. "You could stand to gain a few, you know that?" he whispered, nibbling on her neck.

She pressed her palms against his chest. "When Elizabeth Taylor visited the University of Virginia, she sat on the Jeffries' Duncan Phyfe, and of course, the press photographed her there and—"

"Cupcake"—he held himself above her and stared into her eyes—"I don't care about the damned couch."

"It's a sofa."

"Whatever. I'd like to see you sprawled on it. Naked and waiting."

"Right there in the President's Reception Room? Hardly a private forum."

"I have fond, vivid memories of dropping you to the ground just outside Poplar Forest." She was warm between her legs. Probably wet. He pressed his hard penis to her clothing, feeling her heat. Judging by her strong heart beat against his chest, the desire was reciprocal. "I had my way with you at every plantation remotely related to the Jefferson family. Except Tuckahoe."

"No, Tuckahoe had her way with you, and if you'll excuse me..." She squirmed out from under him. "I need a shower."

All right, maybe he deserved the dig about Tuckahoe. Just before she disappeared behind the bathroom door, he watched her yank out her hair tie. Copper waves crashed against her shoulders. He could almost feel her hair slipping through his fingers, brushing against his chest.

He was in for a wild ride. Now that they'd reunited carnally, he'd schedule daily tumbles with her, find the time to pleasure her amid the hullabaloo of their important task. Where on Jefferson's grounds would he take her first?

The Dome Room. He'd take her up to Monticello's third floor and press her against the west windows, the pink glow of the sunset illuminating her, bringing out the red in her hair. No historian knew for certain what purpose Jefferson had intended with the domed room; rumor had it that the beautiful, well-lit space had become storage by the time of its creator's death.

Well, Scott could certainly stash *something* away there. And T.J., if he were still alive, would probably grin at the thought of it.

*   *   *

"Good morning, Brandywine." Seated at an old rattan table on the back porch across from Dusky, Star sipped chamomile tea from a homemade mug and regarded her daughter with a smile. A wave of pink sparkled in her daughter's aura this morning. "Surprised to see you this early."

Brandywine made her way across the dew-glistening porch and rolled into the cushioned wicker sofa. "I accidentally set my alarm last night after my date."

"New guy?" Dusky asked. "Here, have some tea. Compliments of Susie's Sweets in town."

Brandywine grumbled a negative response.

Star poured her a cup, regardless. "What did Molly have to say last night?"

"Her wedding ring was blue." Brandywine brushed unruly ringlets of hair from her eyes. "It seems the professor of love shot an arrow with perfect aim. Bought her an antique sapphire on the day they said 'I do.' Such a sucker for old things, that girl."

"Tell me about this professor," Dusky said.

"You probably know more about him than I do," the younger woman said with a yawn. "Handsome, almost too pretty, with an ass I'd like to take a bite out of."

Star chuckled.

"Child, we have to teach you to channel all you see." Dusky straightened the white-and-tangerine striped scarf over her coffee-colored curls.

"It's no use, Dusky. I don't have the gift."

"We all have it," Star said. "You have to wait for your time is all."

"You mean I have to wait for the right guy. Do you know how many guys I haven't seen twice due to our family's crazy history? 'Sorry, no uncanny ability. I can't see you again.' It's exhausting—and unfair to the one guy who might actually be the one. How many soul mates do you think I'll be finding in Parker's Landing? I don't have it, I don't want it, and I'm tired of relying on it to point me in the right direction." Brandywine rubbed her eyes, and reached to the table for her tea.

"Finding your soul mate doesn't trigger your ability." Dusky sipped her tea. "Once you're at peace with yourself, when you open your mind and your heart to the possibility of higher thinking, bigger picture issues, you'll come into your own. Look at Molly. She didn't fall in love when she realized her ability to—" She set down her tea. "Well, I guess she did, didn't she? We just didn't know it. But your mother..." Dusky nodded at Star. "She met your father, and nothing changed, but when she learned she was pregnant—"

"You didn't love my father?" Brandywine snapped her gaze to Star.

"No one said that." Star watched her daughter's aura deepen from pink to magenta.

"No one's ever said otherwise."

"Maybe you should go back to bed."

"You see blue when you look at Molly," Brandywine said. "Know what I see? Molly. Of course, lately, I've been picturing her in a hat, but that's probably because I keep getting spam-mail from rat-a-tat-hat-dot-com."

"How did she sound last night?" Star asked.

Brandywine sipped her tea and shrugged. "Tempted."

"That's what I feared." Dusky stirred her tea with a cinnamon stick. "She give in?"

"God, I hope so."

"I don't know." Dusky drummed her fingernails on the tabletop. "That man's got history."

"With a bod like that, who cares about his past? Can you imagine what their children would look like? With Molly's freaky weight control, her hair, his eyes, and his smile? Irish super models."

"Some history isn't worth repeating." Star brushed the gold ring she wore on her index finger. Once upon a time, she'd relied on that ring to carry her through forever. No longer a wedding band, no longer a promise, it still reminded her she could always depend on herself. "Molly's fragile right now."

Brandywine shrugged. "He seemed all right to me."

"Oh, he has the intentions of a saint," Dusky said. "What he's lacking is the follow-through. Take his mama, for instance. The woman didn't know how to use that gun."

The mug slipped from Brandywine's fingers and hit the deck with a thud, breaking off the handle and spilling the hot tea to the floor.

*   *   *

As Molly drove east on Route 64, the heavy mist rolling across the road took her breath away. So beautiful against the red soil of her ex-husband's homeland. Her heart thumped. *Welcome to Virginia, where Professor Sheridan stole my heart—and my peace of mind.*

She shivered and smoothed her hair—pinned in a bun around a rubber band—and took a deep breath. As much as she hated to admit it, she'd worn her hair up because he'd surely want to take it down. She'd met her quota on resisting him today.

"Want some chocolate?" Scott held a tempting chunk of a Three Musketeers bar inches away from her mouth.

Tired of resisting chocolate, too, she opened her mouth in acceptance. He placed the morsel on her tongue. "So good," she murmured, as the chocolate melted over her taste buds and caressed her mouth with delightful, creamy nougat. "Mmm."

He chuckled. "It only takes a candy bar to evoke that sound? I wish someone had told me that a few nights ago."

Maybe she'd over-reacted to a commercial treat wrapped in foil, but it had been months since she'd allowed such a thing in her mouth. She glanced at her ex-husband—below the belt. All right, recently she'd swallowed lots of uncustomary things.

"Want to finish it?"

Did she ever. "No."

"What if I insist?" He broke another piece off and fed her.

"Mmm."

"Lord, I love to watch you enjoy things."

"No more," she said, rolling the chocolate in her mouth. "I can't take it."

"Oh yes, you can."

"Better than sex." Did she say that aloud?

"What? Pull over, so I can prove you wrong."

Apparently so. *To Do List: Tape your mouth shut.*

"If you think this sixty-cent piece of additives and preservatives is better than sex, I didn't do my job last night. Not for lack of trying, Miss Molly. Five times in one night. I think that might be a record."

She tried to hide her smile. "Do we have to talk about it?"

"No."

"It probably shouldn't have happened."

"Then why do we keep talking about it?"

She opened her mouth to rebut, but he didn't give her the chance.

"Hey, we're making good time," he said. "Forget about settling in at the hotel first, and continue east on sixty-four."

"Why?"

"A little something to inspire you. Have you ever seen Monticello in the rain?"

"No."

"It's the most romantic sight you'll ever see. Fog rolling in off the hills, draping over the terraces, and lingering at the piazzas. Imagine the two of us standing on the southwest portico, waiting for the sun to set. A chill in the air, and only me to warm you."

Quite possibly, she'd never wanted to experience anything more. But being alone on Jefferson's "Little Mountain," wrapped in Scott's embrace, had proven dangerous in the past. "I'm tired."

"Not my fault you woke up with the sunshine."

"Not my fault you distracted me all night."

"I'll bet I can get you a sneak peak at the Dome Room, even though it's not open to the public. Never will be on the standard house tour, due to fire codes. But I can probably finagle you a visit. Today. Now. And maybe you'll feel something about the room, about how Jefferson had intended to use it."

He might as well have been dangling another candy bar in front of her mouth, but pressure built in her gut. "What if I don't feel anything?"

He shrugged. "Then I guess your knowledge of couches and easy chairs will have to suffice."

"Sofas."

"Cupcake, I'd like you to stay, regardless of the vibes. I told you that."

"How far is Charlottesville?"

"I don't know." He popped another chunk of chocolate into her mouth. "I've been watching you, not the road."

"And you're wrong," she said. "The night you drew the ten of hearts, and we decided to get married, we did it six times."

"Six times. Not bad."

"Not entirely." *Not at all.*

He shrugged. "I was quite a bit younger back then, but I'll see what I can do to score another personal best."

She passed the exit for the motel at which they'd planned to stay and kept on. Separate, adjoining, or shared rooms, they'd yet to discuss. Shared, her heart and nether-regions prayed, but the logical side of her brain kept those wishes in check.

He opened a Twix and stuck half of it in her mouth. *Sensational.* She savored the crunchy cookie, the caramel, the chocolate, rolling the foreign flavors on her tongue. If she weren't driving, she'd have closed her eyes to make a memory of the taste. "I'd forgotten how good this stuff was."

"I think we'd both forgotten how good things could be." He dropped a hand onto her thigh, and there it remained until a signpost directing them to Monticello emerged through the mist. "All my wishes end where I hope my days will end. At Monticello."

Any random observer would think her ex-husband had merely quoted an influential historical figure, but Molly tuned in not only the words, but the way he'd spoken them. She'd heard that hushed whisper once before.

I, Nathaniel Scott Sheridan, take you, Molly Rourke to be my wife. To have and to hold, for richer, for poorer, in sickness and in health, in good and bad times. Until death parts us.

Or until a disgusting, handmade book turns up in a garden at Tuckahoe Plantation. Whichever.

She parked the car in the visitors' lot.

Hand-in-hand, they began up the walk. Upon first sight of the house, Scott's fingers tensed in her hand, demonstrating the power Jefferson's home held over him. Having lived an hour from the plantation his entire life, and nurturing a love for its history, he must have viewed the mansion hundreds of times. Yet still, when faced with its glory, a somber respect glistened in his eyes.

"What'd I tell you?" he said. "Romance at its best."

"You weren't kidding," she whispered.

Fog hung around the L-shaped terraces, like cotton weaving through the railings, each constructed in a unique design. And while the sight was truly beautiful, utterly romantic, a twinge of jealousy pulled in her gut. Dr. Sheridan would never regard her with the awe with which he had Jefferson's lady.

She let go of his hand; he didn't seem to notice.

Here we go again. Second place to Thomas Jefferson.

No sooner had the thought jumped from one synapse to another, than he disproved it. He slid his arm around her waist and led her to the northeast entrance of Monticello, where a white-haired, female docent from the Thomas Jefferson Foundation greeted them with a smile and a nod. "Dr. Sheridan. I presume you don't need a guide."

Scott smiled in return. "No, I'm all right, Sophie. Thanks." He tipped his head in Molly's direction. "This is Molly Rourke, my furniture expert."

"Where have you been hiding her?" Sophie squeezed her just above the elbow with a gentle, aged hand.

"Chicago."

"First time to Monticello?" the docent asked.

Molly shook her head and followed the pull of Scott's hand over the threshold. "I was here once before." They stepped onto the wooden, grass green floor of the Entrance Hall.

Five years had passed since she'd been here, but time stood still in this architectural monument. Lewis and Clark's diplomatic gifts from Native Americans, maps of westward expansion, and paintings and busts of influential figures made the hall a mini-museum.

Images of another museum and Chagall's blue windows materialized in her mind.

"We all make mistakes," Scott said softly as he turned her toward the clock, which kept track of the day of the week with what appeared to be cannon balls.

Sunday, Monday, Tuesday, Wednesday, Thursday, and Friday were lettered in a ladder formation from ceiling to floor. "Jefferson designed this clock for a home in Philadelphia, where he lived for a short time. When he produced it here, the weight system required more height than this room had to offer, so Saturday is in the basement."

She noted a hole cut into the entrance hall floor to accommodate the balls displaying the last day of the week.

"When in doubt, improvise." He led her toward the north side of the house, although most tours continued either into the parlor on the southwest side of the house or into the south square room. They paused at the foot of a narrow staircase, roped off like an exhibit and guarded by another docent.

"Upper floors are closed to the public, sir."

"I know that." Scott flashed his smile and his ID. "We haven't met yet. I'm Professor Sheridan, with Washington and Lee University, and this is Molly Rourke, my furniture historian. As you know, the quest for the grant starts tomorrow, and she's never seen the third floor."

The docent pulled a walkie-talkie from his belt and raised it to his lips. "Professor Sheridan and his furniture specialist are here, requesting admission to the upper floors."

The muffled approval came through. "Admit him."

The docent nodded at Molly. "Be careful. The stairs are steep."

Scott again took her hand and together they made the mysterious ascent to Monticello's secret levels. "Triple pane skylight." He nodded toward the window in the stairwell. It was closed today due to the rain. "Aids in ventilation. Can you imagine a house of this magnitude built in the nineteenth century? The man was an architectural genius, cupcake. Pure genius. Wouldn't I love to have just one conversation with him. What do you know about channeling? Can you do it?"

"I'm not a sideshow."

"Can you?"

"No!"

"What about Dusky?"

"Until recently, she's never given me an accurate reading, but she works through touch."

"So?"

She followed the pull of his hand and took in every minute detail along the way. Ornate baseboard molding, elaborate entablature on the hallway crown. "Tommy J's hardly available for touching now, is he? Besides, there's a respect issue at hand."

"Respect for the dead?"

"No, a lack of respect for politicians. Dusky wants nothing to do with them."

"Seeing this place, how can you classify this man as anything but an artist, and how can you not respect him?"

"First, I doubt Dusky will ever see this place. She hasn't traveled much further than Wisconsin. She's a homebody, rarely leaves Parker's Landing, where she best connects her root center to the core of the earth. Second, when she pictures Thomas Jefferson, she doesn't consider this house, the Declaration, the University of Virginia, or any of his other gigantic accomplishments. She conjures the man who never admitted to loving a woman he had six children with."

He pulled her close, squeezed both her hands, and brushed a kiss over her lips. "Cupcake?"

She inhaled the faint scent of cinnamon chewing gum on his breath and stared into his mesmerizing green eyes. "Mmm-hmm?"

"What do you think?"

She blinked away to see pale yellow walls and circular windows. "The Dome Room?"

"The one and only." Scott lowered his forehead to hers and backed her toward the center of the room. "Fascinating, isn't it?"

"Gorgeous." But she couldn't focus on the walls surrounding her.

When he stood so close, all she wanted to do was tumble to the ground with him.

"Do you feel anything?" His arms encircled her, his every muscle a comfort. He planted one hand on her rear. "Any vibes?"

She pressed her torso tight to his. "Not a one." But she felt what was important—her ex-husband's body in direct alignment with hers, as if some god had created them to fit together just right.

*   *   *

The bouncing tendril at her temple demanded a fingering. As he touched it, he glanced away from her serious eyes long enough to register the auburn knob atop her head. The bun in her hair, along with the cropped sweater tied over a snug-fitting t-shirt, invoked the image of her on Amelia's maple dance floor in Parker's Landing.

"Suppose I asked you to dance," he whispered.

She blinked up at him, but quickly averted her gaze. In doing so, she awarded him a glimpse of the freckles peeking through powder on the bridge of her nose. "You want to dance?"

"No. I want to watch you dance, the way you did back in that studio."

"That wasn't dancing, as much as it was stretching."

"Whatever it was, I liked it." He pulled a hairpin from her bun and twirled it between his fingers as if it were a miniature baton. "Show me."

"No."

"Yes." He kissed her forehead.

"There's a houseful of tourists downstairs."

"No one's up here."

Pluck, pluck, pluck.

He pulled hairpins from her hair and kissed her once on each cheek and once on her mouth.

"Don't take my hair down."

He inhaled its lilac scent. "You don't sound convincing, and I can't help myself."

Pluck.

Kiss.

"Try."

"Dance."

Their gazes met and she straightened. "When Elizabeth Taylor visited the University of Virginia, she sat on the Duncan Phyfe sofa,

71

and the media photographed her there. Needless to say, the Jeffries family then knew someone had sat on their look-at donation, and the university had reupholstered it. Both no-nos."

"So they broke both rules." He cupped her soft chin in his hand and lowered his mouth to hers. "Shame on them."

"Yes," Molly whispered into his kiss.

And shame on him for wasting five years of what could have been their life together. "Do you ever think about things, Miss Molly?" he asked against her lips. "About us? About what we could have been?"

"Yes."

He nibbled an earlobe, heard her heavy exhalation, and felt her relax against his chest. "We were good together, weren't we?" He extracted another pin from her hair.

"Yes."

"We were pretty good last night."

"Yes."

"Think we can be that good again?"

"Yes."

"Lord, I want you saying 'yes' for the next few decades."

"Excuse me," came a voice from the hallway.

Startled, Scott dropped the hairpins to the floor and turned to acknowledge Stacie Wilkinson, clad in a double-breasted pants suit.

"Wilkinson," he said.

"Sheridan." She turned to his ex-wife, who had crouched to gather the scattered pins and had begun shoving them back into her bun. "And you must be the ex-missus." She offered her hand. "Dr. Stacie Wilkinson. University of Virginia."

"Molly Rourke. Vaughan Appraisals." She stuffed the last hairpin into a mass of curls and gave Stacie's hand a hearty shake as she stood. "Scott was just showing me—"

"The Dome Room. I know. Stunning view." Stacie turned to him. "Could've bet a hundred to one she'd be a redhead. And not just any red—Jefferson Red."

Scott grabbed Molly by the elbow before she could walk away. "If you'll excuse us, Wilkinson, we were in the middle of something."

"Obviously something quite professional from my vantage point."

"Worry about your own team, and I'll worry about mine."

"Believe it or not, I'm here as a courtesy. To welcome you in the name of good sportsmanship."

Good sportsmanship, his eye. She'd come for a gander at her

competition.

"I was having a cup of coffee downstairs with the curator when your request for admittance came through, so I thought I'd say a formal hello. Now that I have, carry on. Welcome to Virginia, Ms. Rourke." With that, Wilkinson pivoted out of the Dome Room.

He shoved his hands through his hair. *Coffee with the curator in Monticello's staff-only quarters.* That was all he needed—his rival buddying up with the one gal who could reward him the opportunity of a lifetime. Not that he'd have a leg up now that Molly hadn't gauged a damn iota about the history of the Dome Room. Perhaps it was his fault, since he had distracted her.

He headed out the door, following in his competitor's wake. It wasn't until he felt Molly's soft hand in his grasp that he realized she'd left the room with him.

"Are you all right?" she asked.

"What? Yeah." He curled his fingers around hers.

"Scottie, about the hotel situation…"

"What about it? I told you we'd do whatever you want. Separate, adjoining…whatever you're most comfortable with."

"Actually I was wondering if you have any family nearby. A month is a long time to rent a room, don't you think?"

A month. So she was just as determined as he to battle Wilkinson for the grant. His cheeks grew warm, and he clamped his mouth shut, swallowing hard. "No family in Charlottesville."

"Any near the Rappahannock?"

At the top of the flight of stairs, he squeezed her hand. "Why the Rappahannock?"

"I don't know, a little town called Port Royal, maybe?"

He began the descent. "There are dozens of other towns in Virginia."

"I know, but—"

"Yes, ma'am, I had family in Port Royal."

"There are libraries near Port Royal, aren't there?"

"I know where this is going." He sighed. "Some other time, all right?"

"When I'm well on my way back to Chicago maybe?"

"We have a long day tomorrow. I think we'd best settle in to discuss our game plan for the mysterious Dome Room. We're assuming we'll get the chance to present next month, but in order to do that, we have to make the cut tomorrow."

"Lover's retreat."

"What?"

"That's it. A lover's retreat..." She took a deep breath and looked away before meeting his glance.

"I knew you could do it," he whispered.

"It isn't a vibe, it's an idea, but bear with me. Given the European influence of the home, and the romance generally associated with places like Paris, Rome, Madrid...all places Jefferson admired architecturally, it makes sense that his Monticello would have a romantic getaway all its own. Where better than the Dome Room? The most distinct, arguably, of all rooms in this country?"

He propped a foot on a stair and peered up at her. "Keep going."

"Correct me if I'm wrong, but I think he'd have books in any room he frequented. Maybe those of the lighter variety up here. French prose. Poetry. A volume or two placed on a Hepplewhite side table, for quick reference in quoting. And maybe he'd enjoy the company of a lady from time to time. Away from his private apartment downstairs, where he'd undoubtedly be interrupted by his daughter, or even, occasionally, guests, servants, what-have-you."

He kneaded her hand in encouragement. "Are we talking about a hideaway for Ms. Hemings?"

"Yes. No. I don't know, but it's passionate in there."

"Quite."

"Of course, maybe that was you. Us, I mean."

He grinned.

"That came out wrong."

"Well, let's make it come out right then, shall we?" He pulled a pin from her hair and dragged it across her lips.

"South of the Honeymoon Gazebo. This place, our past—"

"How many more pins do you have stashed away in there?" He nodded toward her bun.

"Seventeen."

"In that case, you owe me seventeen kisses. Shared room?"

CHAPTER 7

"The past two nights have been amazing," Molly whispered into her cell phone. She stood in the library lobby at the University of Virginia. Just inside the double doors, she'd been compiling notes on furniture pieces of distinction.

"Amen to amazing," Brandywine said.

"Amen to nothing! Do you know how close I am to drowning in the scent of his cinnamon gum? We were up all night formulating a proposal, and this morning we successfully beat out ten other academic teams, including Georgetown, and three corporations. And we did it together. Do you know how dangerous this is? We're brilliant in the bedroom, magnificent in the boardroom, and I can't do this again, Brandy. I can't fall for him twice."

"Maybe you aren't falling *for* him. Maybe you're falling *on* him. And that's all right, too."

"We're *good* together…that doesn't make us *right* together."

"Meet his family yet?"

A familiar emptiness settled in her gut. "You know, I assumed once I'd married a man I wouldn't have the anxiety of meeting the parents, but it's forever hanging over me."

"Dusky mentioned something the other day that gave me the willies. Ask him about his mother's shooting skills."

"Shooting skills?"

"Hey, I don't know a thing, and Dusky's not explaining. She says she doesn't use her gift for gossip."

"Are you kidding? When was the last time you saw any of them using it for the good of mankind? All they ever do is gossip about it." Out of the corner of her eye, Molly saw Professor Wilkinson approaching in a hounds-tooth pattern business suit that screamed professionalism.

Molly looked down at her leotard and roll-down tights. *Small town, wanna-be ballerina.* Spending her days poking around attics and antique warehouses in the Midwest, she hadn't needed more formal clothing, but it seemed necessary here. She'd already exhausted her business wardrobe at the preliminary presentation that morning.

To do list: Shop for an appropriate ensemble in which to present to the curator next month.

Molly slipped back into the stacks, hid behind a book shelf, and perused some titles. "Gotta run, Brandy. I'll call you later."

Wilkinson walked past the row, yet just when Molly thought she was home-free—

"Interesting subject matter." The click of Wilkinson's heels halted behind her.

Damn.

"Are you lost?"

"No." Molly unclenched her teeth, turned toward her, and forced a smile. "Mysticism happens to fascinate me. Meditation, holistic healing…"

"Hmm." With crossed arms, her rival leaned against a bookshelf. "I'll bet you need all the healing you can get with that clown on your tail. He's exhausting, isn't he?"

Lately, it was the constant sexual activity exhausting her. The man only made it possible. Although it probably shouldn't have happened, probably couldn't continue if she expected to keep her sanity—and her heart in one piece. "I suppose I should congratulate you on making it to the finals." Molly shoved a curl from her forehead. "Looks like it's just us. Head to head."

"Where's Sheridan?" Wilkinson studied her manicure. "I'd like to extend a few congratulations of my own."

"Presently, he's renting a studio at the Residence Inn. Since we'll be here for a few weeks, we're settling in."

"Playing house again?"

"I'm sorry?"

"That's all that man does." At last, Wilkinson awarded her the courtesy of eye contact. "Play."

"I didn't realize the two of you were well acquainted."

"We did our undergrad together. Believe me, I did you a favor when I made that call."

Molly pushed at a loose pin in her hair. "I beg your pardon? Call?"

"The journal found at Tuckahoe."

"I hadn't realized—"

"It was perfect, if I do say so. He raced home to have a look at what I'd already determined was a fake. One good turn deserves another, I always say. You don't marry one gal when you're playing with another, but no harm, no foul. I love a little healthy competition."

No harm, no foul? Healthy competition? "He never mentioned dating anyone when we met. Are you sure we're talking about the right man?"

"Scott Sheridan isn't right for anyone, and you'd be playing it fast and loose with the term 'dating,' but don't worry about it. Bygones."

"Bygones? This is the dissolution of my marriage we're talking about."

"For which you ought to thank me. So what's your game plan for the Dome?"

Now Molly knew there was a personal stake in the game, her plan was to bury Wilkinson's team in seconds flat. "What's yours?"

"I'm not at liberty to say, but it doesn't matter, does it? You and I both know Jefferson's own university has this one in the bag." She shrugged. "Political bonds."

"Professor Wilkinson, I, too, enjoy a little healthy competition. And I'm willing to wager my ex-husband against your title as UVA's history department chair."

Wilkinson pursed her lips and straightened. "I don't want your ex-husband."

"I don't want your job, but winner keeps what she does want." Assuming, of course, she wanted what she'd wagered. Which she didn't. Not really. Not entirely. All right, she did.

"Then I'd say you're wasting your time here in the mystic section of my library." Wilkinson began to walk away. "You'd best get back to work."

"Oh, hadn't you guessed?" Molly pulled a book entitled *The Hauntings of Albemarle County* from a shelf and opened it to a random page. "I'm confident with our plan. I have time for all the hobbies in the world. Meditation, aphrodisiac cooking...and toying with Scott Sheridan."

"May the best collegiate empire take all, in that case."

It wasn't until Wilkinson's footsteps faded that Molly registered what she'd been staring at on the pages of the random book: a local historian of the paranormal…seated on a Chippendale side chair.

*　　*　　*

Scott paced the hotel terrace and checked his watch again. Where the hell was Molly? She'd planned to pick him up before returning to Monticello. Their appointment in the Dome Room was in less than an hour. She hadn't answered her cell phone when he'd attempted to reach her. Suppose she'd gotten lost on her way to the new hotel, traveled out of cellular service? Or maybe she was hurt.

He tucked a hand into his trouser pocket and grasped her wedding ring. If something had happened to her, he'd like to think he'd feel some sort of dissonance, the way he had when his mother had died. But over the years, he'd felt only a vague disappointment whenever he thought about Molly. Disappointment in his failure to hold onto her. Disappointment in the fact he'd probably never see her again. Disappointment in his never telling her the truth about how he felt.

This was his second chance, an opportunity to make things right. He leaned against the railing and studied the breathtaking horizon. Jefferson had inherited his land from his Randolph relatives, in much the same way Scott had acquired the deed to his parents' acreage, Honey Hill. There had been a time he'd equated beginning a life with Molly Rourke to Jefferson's building Monticello. A new, passionate quest, knowing the end result could be superb. But a ratty, old book— not to mention the previous tainting of Honey Hill's soil—had put a premature stop to reaching the pot of gold.

The jingling of keys and the rattling of the doorknob whisked him from his reverie. "Gracie." Molly's voice sounded strained. "Help me out, just this once."

With a smile too pure to hide, he walked through the room and opened the door to find her arm stuck through the pierced back of an old chair, car keys dangling between her teeth, her arms laden with half a dozen plastic shopping bags, and the hotel key card, sticking haphazardly out of the lock.

"Oh, cupcake, you bought a chair for our new home." He gently removed the chair from its position and carried it past the threshold.

"No, I chased halfway across Albemarle County for it. Dumb luck. I saw it in a book about local hauntings, called my dad for a favor—

turns out he once met the historian who owned it—and the second I touched it, I knew. It's an original." She unloaded the bags onto the luggage rack.

"Where was it? Originally, I mean."

"Try Williamsburg. George Wythe House. Its previous owner claims it was one of the items thrown down the stairs during a rather...inexplicable occurrence."

"You're kidding."

"I never kid about furniture. Or ghosts. I thought we'd offer it to the curator. Kind of a 'thanks for the opportunity' gift."

"She'll cream her jeans when you tell her where it used to be."

"I can't do that. I have no proof."

"So it wasn't at the George Wythe House?"

"Oh, it was there, all right, and T.J. himself settled into that baby from time to time. But I can't tell her something I *feel* and expect her to believe in my credibility as an antiquities expert."

"So just stick with 'it's an original,' right?" He opened a bag. "A scale?"

"Yes, a scale. I've been eating like it's the Last Supper."

"Good, you need it."

"Oh, I know what I need, and two thousand calories a day doesn't even make the top ten."

He pulled her close, waltzed her to the donated chair and settled her onto it while he knelt between her legs, worked his hands up her thighs, and leaned into her lips for a kiss. "What is this obsession with calories?"

She blew curls out of her eyes and reciprocated with a kiss of her own. "What is it with Professor Wilkinson and games?"

His hands had reached her hips, and he kneaded with his thumbs inches away from parts that would entice the sweetest moans. "I don't think I heard you."

"Stacie Wilkinson. Games."

"I was trying to change the subject." He swept his tongue over a soft part of her neck. "We were picking up speed there for a few moments."

"Unless you're talking about research, speed's the last thing we need."

"Too late, we're already running."

"We should stop." Her whisper wasn't nearly as convincing as she'd hoped.

"Stop me then." He suckled a fleshy earlobe. *Delicious.*

"Ohhhh." A slight quiver ran through her, a flattering review of his efforts. "You were dating her when you married me."

"Until I met you. There's a difference."

"She called you back home for the Tuckahoe find." Her words were little more than a gruff whisper, and her tongue moistening her lips could only mean good things for him.

He nodded, his groin aching to feel something wet, taut, and intense. He peeled her leotard off her shoulders—"I know what you're thinking, but it wasn't like that"—and melted a kiss onto her collarbone. Lord, there was no mediocre place to plant his mouth on the woman. He trailed kisses down one arm as he pulled off the dancewear.

"It's ancient history, but I deserve to know. Did you leave me for her?"

He shook his head against her cotton bra; a sharp intake of air answered his feathering caresses. "You're not the kind of woman a man leaves for whimsical reasons." He popped the clasp. Her firm breasts filled his hands and successfully sprung him to full-mast below the belt. "Molly, Molly, Molly."

"What anti-whimsy took you away?" she said against his lips. "Why not take me with you?"

His heart clanged with both passion and avoidance, while he prepared to read her the line he'd practiced years ago. "We didn't kn—"

"Don't tell me we didn't know one another well enough to leave our lives behind." She raised his chin with a gentle index finger. "The second we met, a decade passed. I didn't imagine it, and neither did you."

He squeezed a thigh and refused to stray from her gaze.

"And it happened again the moment you walked into Amelia's."

"Something like that," he whispered.

"I'd have followed you anywhere."

"You'd have watched me fail."

"It would have been my pleasure."

He lowered his mouth to her breasts. "I'll take you to Port Royal," he whispered against her flesh. "After the project's pitched. I'll show you failure." *And what's left of my past.*

He laved her nipples with his tongue, and she arched into him. "Monticello's gates lock in forty-five minutes," she said. "Got your notes?"

"I've got notes, all right. Notes on how to make you squeal."

"Scottie, no." She pushed against his shoulders, which sent him stumbling to the floor. Before he regained his bearings, she'd climbed on top of him. "That chair's an antique. We couldn't possibly—"

He wove a hand into the straying tendrils at the nape of her neck, kissed her into silence, and began to work off her clothing. Her hand wiggled into his pants, and she stroked him thoroughly from base to tip. A guttural groan escaped him, along with a drop of pre-ejaculation. "No time for me," he said, scooting downward, yanking the leotard over her hips. "No panties?"

"I don't wear panties with this—Ohhh."

He flattened his tongue against her hard clitoris, and licked and nibbled and sucked at her until she took matters into her own hands.

*   *   *

For the sake of her sanity, she ought to have denied him. She could almost feel the blue crustacean hardening in her aura, but she was powerless to resist him. He felt too good. He knew too well how to heighten each and every one of her senses. He was like chocolate—so good, and so bad for her.

She rocked on his mouth, maneuvering his teasing tongue deep into the crevice between her legs. Before long, she tensed atop him, on the verge of orgasm. *So good.* She trapped her clit between two fingers, and the friction, combined with the talent of his tongue, carried her over the edge.

*   *   *

"Her elation won't last," Star said, lifting a shot of wheatgrass in salute. "Unless they overcome a huge obstacle.

"I'm telling you, Star, they'll overcome it." Brandywine clinked glasses and threw back the shot. "She isn't coming home."

"She'll be home." Star sipped the beverage, savoring it the way she always did. A lesson in pacing the intake of nourishment. Over-indulgence was a hard habit to break. "She knows where she belongs, and her heart may yearn for Virginia, and whoever keeps a home there, but she'll bloom where she was planted. Like the rest of us."

"So she's destined to spend the rest of her life with a blue calcification? Cruel gods. Shoot." She tapped the heel of her hand to her forehead. "Speaking of gods, I was supposed to rub Chubs for luck."

"Your cousin doesn't need luck, Brandywine. What she needs is to slow down long enough to gauge her desires. She's jumped into the deep end of the ocean with this man again, and she doesn't know where he's come from."

"She's working on that one. Besides, he isn't a stranger. He's her husband."

"One and the same, Brandy." Star felt a headache coming on, which was never a good sign. She wouldn't sleep well tonight. There were just too many unsettled thoughts weaseling into her mind. Most of which she couldn't decipher. What good was knowing Scott had found his dead mother with a gun in her hand, if Star was in no position to help? She took another sip. "I don't doubt they can be very, very good together, but two trains rushing toward each other are only going to crash."

"You know what happened, don't you?"

Star licked wheatgrass from her lips. "I have a pretty good idea."

"Devil's advocate. Why can't you fill Molly in?"

"I can. I think it'll do more harm than good, coming from me."

"Can't you drop a hint or two?"

"If I knew which hints to drop, I would. It's what's been keeping me up at night."

Brandywine rinsed her glass in the farm sink and blew a kiss. "I'll be home early tonight."

"New guy?" Star asked.

Her daughter smiled. "Get some sleep, will you? Molly's got it all under control."

*   *   *

With the setting sun behind them, Scott drove through Monticello's gates, while from the passenger seat, Molly attempted to shake the heat periodically crawling into her cheeks. *After-effects of an orally stimulated orgasm, perhaps?* God, the man was amazing with his tongue. Was she distracted due to the promise she'd soon see Honey Hill in Port Royal? Or perhaps because she knew he'd never make good on such a pledge? "We're so late."

"Five minutes." Scott checked the rearview mirror. "Hey, do me a favor. Eat something."

"I'm fine."

"Your stomach hasn't stopped growling since your thighs put a vice grip on my head."

"We'll grab some takeout on the way back to the hotel."

"There's a granola bar in my briefcase. Eat it."

"If I know you, it isn't so much a granola bar as it is peanut butter and chocolate chips, and I need neither." She rustled around and peered into his briefcase, if only to confirm her suspicions, and yanked out the bar in question. "How well do I know you?"

"Eat it. You could use a little peanut butter on those bones."

"First, there's plenty on these bones. Second, I don't like peanut butter."

"You seemed to like it just fine the day I smeared it across your belly."

"I've learned to live without a lot of things since then. Peanut butter's one of them. You're another."

With a grin designed to entice the thumping of her heart, he squeezed her knee and parked at the visitor's center. "You've got me now, don't you?"

She'd certainly had him in bed a few times, but that wasn't the same as owning someone. She unwrapped the "granola" candy bar and took a bite. Why did everything taste so god-awful good in the presence of her ex-husband? And why did she succumb to every temptation? If she shifted in the seat, her still-engorged nether regions surged with numb pleasure, reminding her of his most recent persuasion in the bedroom. She bit another chunk off the bar and accompanied him out of the car.

Alive with activity, the carriage entrance to Monticello appeared when they climbed up the hill. Scott nodded toward a group of seven coeds in Washington and Lee History Club windbreakers huddled in a circle to the left of the door. "My students."

"Students? We're meeting students?"

"No pressure. But if we win the grant, they'll be working here next semester. And if we don't, they'll most likely never have a chance to wander the upper floors of this place. So either way, I thought it best to involve them in the steps along the way."

She licked the last morsel of chocolate from her lips and glanced down at her outfit: blue jazz pants, leather clogs, and the college sweatshirt Scott had worn earlier. *Nothing like making the wrong impression.* She fiddled with what was left of her hairpins, as half of them had fallen to the thin hotel carpeting during their rendezvous. "I thought we were here to size up the oculus."

He gave a quick nod. "And to see what my students have to say about our plan."

Her heartbeat filled her ears the way overtly scary music pre-empted doom in bad horror flicks. "I smell like sex."

"So do I." He shot her with a bright-green-eyed stare and grinned. "Stop fussing. You look great."

"I look like I just—"

His kiss shut her up, and his hands tangled in her hair, yanking at the pins and scrunching her curls. "There. *Now* you look like you just."

She followed the pull of his hand toward the students' circle, her hair an unruly mass. "Sorry we're late," he said, nodding toward the door. "Who wants the privileged view from the Dome Room? By the way, this is my wife, Molly Rourke."

If her head could have whipped around any faster, it would have snapped off her neck, but he seemed as unfazed by her reaction to his eliminating the "ex"—again—as he was by the students' following without banter—and during their semester break, no less.

"Molly is a furniture historian," he said as they passed through the doors, "and she has some knock-down ideas for our proposal in this pretty little head of hers."

"Rourke," one student said, jotting in her notebook. "Any relation to the famed Joseph and Windmere?"

"Famed?" Molly asked. "In which social circles?"

Scott leaned to whisper in her ear. "My students—at least this group—view pop-culture historians as a grade of celebrity."

"They were showcased on the History Channel last month," the student said, pen poised and eyes blinking impatiently.

"They're my parents," Molly said.

"We have clearance to the Dome only tonight." Scott nodded hello to the docent guarding the north staircase and took the stairs. "UVA's team is occupying the second floor and the remaining rooms on the third. As tempting as it may be to roam, stay with our group. We'll have our chance to study the entire estate over the next few weeks."

In silence, the students took notes en route down the Central Passage to the Dome Room. Once inside, they followed their professor's lead around the perimeter of the room, each gazing out the circular windows with awed respect. After completing a full circle, Scott directed the group, by example, to plop down in the center of the room, directly beneath the oculus.

"Lie down, if you'd like," he said. "Have a look straight through to heaven, if you believe in that sort of thing. You don't think I passed through this room the first time without doing it, do you?" He lowered his forehead to Molly's and zapped her with his emerald gaze. "Any questions?"

"How long have you been married?" a female student asked.

"Seems like just yesterday, doesn't it, Miss Molly?"

"Sometimes," Molly answered.

"Now." Scott pulled away but curled his fingers around her hand. "Any questions about the room?"

"There are reports that one of Jefferson's grandsons used this room as a bedroom," a male student said.

"Yes, Travis. For a short while."

"So why a mysterious lover's retreat? Why not keep it a bedroom?"

"A: Jefferson was a mysterious man when it came to the lovers he kept. And B: there are two bedrooms on the standard tour. And every room intended to be a bedroom has a bed alcove built into it, which tells me that, while Jefferson may not have known what to do with this space, he never intended it as sleeping quarters.

"Remember, people, the idea isn't to prove our theory, locked and loaded. It's to prove the likelihood of it. And to showcase as many period pieces as we possibly can, which is why we need Molly. This room is an interior specialist's Eden."

One by one, hands popped up, and Scott answered questions in order. Always with an even tone, never superior.

Molly imagined him conducting class in courtyards between old, red-bricked buildings. He probably made magic of humdrum historical subjects. Glasses perched on the edge of his nose, his thumb tucked into some volume or ancient diary, while he gnawed on cinnamon gum. In his element, he was nothing short of astonishing.

And there was no way—on this plane or any other—Molly could keep him from excelling at what he did best, where he was meant to do it. She withdrew from the circle and proceeded to the south side of the Dome Room, into a room informally known as the "cuddy." Although it was little more than attic space accessible only through the Dome Room, Jefferson's granddaughters had written about using the cuddy as private space in which to read and write.

This was where the Washington and Lee team would shelve rare books. *This* was where they'd tuck a lover's sofa, or perhaps a *tête à tête*. A hideaway within a hideaway.

The floor of the cuddy felt warm against her hands, and the setting sun shot through the half-moon window in the tiny alcove. She lifted her face to the rays and took a deep breath. So tired of being blue.

Oh, for heaven's sake, Chubs, I've been a good girl. Give me a break. Good karma, good karma.

CHAPTER 8

Monticello at dawn's first light personified magic. Molly walked along the south terrace, with only the fragrance of Jefferson's gardens for company. Virginia mornings could be cool in spring, and this one was no exception.

Wife. The word haunted her worse than any ghost her parents chased halfway around the world to document. Worse than the oftentimes eerie happenings in her attic dance studio back home. The percentage of her life spent as a wife didn't amount to beans, yet Scott had tossed the term to his students as if he'd been introducing her as his wife every day for the past five years.

And what scared her was that she wished it were true. If anyone had asked her a month ago—which, of course, no one would have asked about what no one knew—she'd have said something along the lines of "Sure, I think about him, but I don't miss him." But now... How could she carry on without him after tasting him once again?

And talk about taste! Chocolate was delicious. A few bites of it, and already, her thighs felt bulky, and her abdomen pooched. Just the thought of the several candy bars she'd ingested over the past few days was enough to turn her stomach.

After the divorce, she'd prided herself on not turning to the comforts of cheesy mashed potatoes, meat loaf, and her aunt's homemade bread to keep it together. Food meant gratification, but she'd had enough pleasure during her twenty-nine days with the gorgeous professor.

However, she wasn't resisting much these days. She must re-learn self-control. In regards to Scott's sweet treats...and chocolate.

"Miss Rourke, good morning."

Molly turned to see Stacie Wilkinson, clad in jeans and a tailored blazer. Jeez, the woman wore dungarees better than Molly wore her Sunday best. "Good morning, Dr. Wilkinson."

"Breathtaking, isn't it?" Wilkinson propped her well-manicured hands on her hips, faced Mulberry Row, and stared across the grounds. "Jefferson was an early riser, did you know that?"

Scott used to chatter incessantly about things like that, but Molly couldn't remember whether he'd mentioned Jefferson's sleeping habits.

The breeze feathered through Wilkinson's short, chestnut bob, leaving Molly to wonder whether the historian's hair had ever been longer. Must have been, knowing Scott's hair fetish.

"He'd walk the terraces in the morning, and often the gardens." Wilkinson sighed. "Amazing to think we're walking the same hallowed ground, isn't it? If Jefferson were here today, he'd be doing exactly what we're doing at this moment."

God, she's in love with Jefferson, too. Short hair or not, Stacie Wilkinson and Scott Sheridan belonged together, if only for the sheer coincidence.

"Of course," Wilkinson continued, "if he were here today, we certainly wouldn't be. He demanded solitary time, and those lucky enough to be graced with his presence respected his wishes."

Molly crossed her arms over her chest—barely there next to Wilkinson's round, generous bosoms—and gazed out over the property. "Cold today."

"Imagine it on New Year's Day, 1772." Wilkinson nudged past Molly. "Before the main house was constructed, Jefferson brought his bride—"

"To the Honeymoon Gazebo."

Wilkinson's brow knit. "No, to the South Pavilion." She pointed to the same building to which Molly had referred, the same building Scott had pressed her up against five years ago. The first place they'd made love as a married couple.

"I can understand why you might refer to it the way you do," the professor of history said. "I suppose you're technically correct, from a layman's point of view."

"Actually, those are Scott's words."

"Like I said." Wilkinson grinned. "Layman."

For a moment, Molly chewed her lip in deliberation, but when she spoke, a confidence she didn't feel laced her words: "The reference is personal. We made a few memories of our own at that pavilion." She brushed past Wilkinson and continued along the terrace.

"Going there now?"

"Yes, if you'll excuse me."

"There are ghosts down there. Aren't you terrified?"

Molly shook her head. "I grew up with ghosts."

"I'm not talking about poltergeists, Ms. Rourke. I'm talking about personal demons. Memories."

"Then I suppose the terror would be personal, wouldn't it?" Molly bobbed a toe against the red, wooden slats of the terrace and, in her best imitation of Aunt Star, raised an eyebrow. When her rival did not respond, she twirled back toward the pavilion.

Just when she was about to pat herself on the back for getting the last word in, however, she realized the truth of Wilkinson's words. *Memories.* The place squirmed with them, but, then again, the entire state of Virginia crawled with reminiscences of a man who'd left her faster than she could sneeze.

God bless you, Professor Wilkinson...you're good at what you do. Wasn't it enough Scott had more of a history with Wilkinson than he did Molly? Did Molly really have to crumble at the woman's feet, running away from memories, too? Absolutely not, although at the moment, the thought had more appeal than reincarnating the terrible end of her passionate past.

She pivoted to the southwest and followed the L-shaped terrace to the Honeymoon Gazebo. Damned if she'd call it anything else, even if the term made her sound like an amateur.

A few hundred yards later, she touched the red brick of the gazebo with trembling fingers. So much had happened in the one-room outbuilding historically speaking, but Molly couldn't remember much of what Scott had told her years ago. Lucky for her, she didn't have to rely on her memory to see the past. She closed her eyes and took it all in with a deep breath.

Books. Books were in abundance here. A young man had studied law, using this pavilion as an office. Not Jefferson, himself, and not a blood relative, but someone close. An in-law maybe.

Music, dancing. A love affair had flared to life just inside the cold walls, and the flaming fireplace did little to warm the lovers, next to the heat of their passion.

There. She opened her eyes. No demons, if not for the surging readiness between her legs.

She glanced down at the soil below, and visions of a mystical connection consumed her. She and Scott. Entwined, needing, fulfilling.

So she'd always want her ex-husband sexually. *Big surprise.* However, the aching in her heart told another story—one undefined, mysteriously blue, and permanently etched inside her. She and Scott. In love.

Damn it, she still loved him, and—*thank you, Stacie Wilkinson*—a trip to the gazebo was just what she'd needed to confirm her suspicion. She leaned against the building and pinched her eyes shut, as if she might will the ache away.

A shrill whistle commanded her attention and she turned to see Scott, strolling toward her. "Remind me to kiss you later," he said.

Kiss me now, if you'd like.

"You're good, cupcake. The Chip and Dale chair was a hit."

"Chippendale."

"Isn't that what I said? They're going to display it in the basement exhibit room until the upper floors are ready. And then it'll find a permanent home up there."

She smiled, although she knew it was a weak one.

"Guess what I just got?" His smile brightened his eyes. "Key to the graveyard gate. Care to chase a few ghosts?"

"Pardon me?"

"Don't tell me you haven't considered it. Ghosts at Monticello?"

She nodded. "There are ghosts here, all right."

*　　　*　　　*

Why did the air always seem cooler inside cemetery gates? Death was cold, there was no doubt about it, but did the sun cease to warm headstones the way it warmed a smiling face?

A simple obelisk marked Jefferson's grave, although the man deserved something much more grandiose than hard, honed granite. Hell, Scott had entombed his mother's body in an elaborate mausoleum facing the Rappahannock River, and while she'd been a great mother, all she'd done for society was add another tick-mark in the abused spouse column.

What a task for an eighteen-year-old kid—burying his mother. His sister Renee had been the eldest at twenty-three, and then Hannah at twenty. But Scott, feeling responsible, had followed Southern tradition.

Planning a funeral was no job for a lady, and he was the oldest, and the only, male heir to Honey Hill.

There had been obstacles with the church, rules about glorifying death—and punishing suicide. The priest had tried to convince him a closed casket and short mass were enough to honor the woman who had birthed him. After all, his mother was more than a victim of suicide, more than an abused wife. She was also—as the State of Virginia had concluded within hours of her death—a murderess.

As Scott saw it, his father had gotten what he deserved. Nathaniel Scott Sheridan III was spending eternity scattered on the floor of the pony stable at Honey Hill. The man had hated horses.

Scott shoved his hand into his pocket, feeling for Molly's ring. When he didn't find it, he tried the other pocket to no avail and desperately reached for the ten-of-hearts in his back pocket, which wasn't there either because he'd changed trousers at the last moment, when Molly pointed out the chocolate stain on the right thigh hadn't come out in the wash. *Oh, hell.*

"You're awfully quiet," she whispered.

"Revered location."

In lieu of her wedding band, he reached for her. He held her body tight; she rested her head against his chest.

"He waited until the Fourth of July to die. He'd slipped in and out of consciousness. Waiting." When Scott closed his eyes, he pictured the plaque at his mother's burial site. *Ellie Sue Sheridan. Devoted mother. May 14, 1947- July 4, 1990.*

Had she waited for the fourth to declare her independence, too?

If so, he'd been a soldier in her private revolution. He'd armed her with the illegal revolver that had ultimately sealed her fate.

"Seen enough?" He patted Molly's backside and pulled away from her.

"We haven't gone back by—"

"Look around all you'd like, and lock up when you're done. I'll meet you in the exhibit room." He tossed her the key ring and started toward the gate. "In the basement. Know where it is?"

"Scottie, I'll—"

"If you get lost, ask a volunteer."

"Wait, I'll go with you."

"Take your time. Mill around."

"Wait. I can't lock that gate."

He stopped, shoving his hands through his hair. She caught up with him and touched him gently on the elbow. The last thing he wanted to do was look at her—he couldn't afford to explain what had rattled him—but her fingers kneaded his flesh in a gentle persuasion.

She handed over the key. "What happened in there?"

"I get uneasy in graveyards."

With a raised eyebrow, she stared up at him as he locked the gate. "You took me to Arlington Cemetery as an engagement gift."

"Arlington's different. Massive. Monumental. This is suffocating."

She nodded. "He's like a father to you." Her words were soft, but certain.

"Who? Jefferson?" He pocketed the key and shook his head. "My father was nothing like Jefferson."

"*Was*? He's gone?"

"Long gone."

"I'm sorry." She took his hand. "What was he like?"

He yanked his hand from her grasp and quickened his pace toward the mansion. Her footsteps scurried behind him.

"Scottie—"

"I don't talk about my father."

"You don't talk about anyone close to you."

He momentarily pinched his eyes shut, and when he opened them again, he focused on the domed top of Jefferson's masterpiece. *Eye on the prize.*

"I don't know you, do I?" She grabbed his elbow and swung her tiny body into his path.

*   *   *

When he looked down at her, she saw a melancholy expression in his face, an extension of the weird vibe she'd registered at the gravesite. She reached to touch his cheek, but he flinched away.

"We have work to do, Ms. Rourke."

"Ms. Rourke?" She again stepped into his path and propped a fist on her hip. "Look, I know what it feels like to live without parents. For as long as I can remember, my parents have been chasing spiritual beings in places of historical significance, and believe me, you don't bring a toddler along for the ride."

"Molly, we—"

"I live in the house my grandparents raised me in, and when they died, I mourned them as if they'd created me, so don't you dare assume I won't understand whatever it is you're going through."

At last he looked down at her. "Who says I'm 'going through' anything?"

"This whole place screams of memories that scare the hell out of me, Scottie. I understand being afraid of the past."

"I'm not afraid of the past. We have work to do." He stepped around her and continued up the hill.

"You're hiding something from me," she called after him. "I can feel it."

*   *   *

Molly stuffed dirty laundry into pillow cases. She hadn't said a word unrelated to work to him since he'd lost it at Jefferson's gravesite. He owed her an apology—and an explanation—but if he could make nice another way, he'd gladly do so.

"I'm almost done with this section." He drummed his fingers against an amber page of Jefferson's correspondence. "He makes mention of the Dome in this letter to Charles Yancey."

"Fascinating." She blinked away from his gaze and reached for the pair of khakis he'd worn earlier, now draped on the back of his chair.

He leaned against the pants, trapping them, and grinned up at her.

"Do you mind?" She yanked the garment out from beneath his shoulder.

"If you can wait ten minutes, I'll go with you."

"No need to interrupt your research, professor. I've been doing laundry for decades. Besides, nothing should come between you and your precious Jeffersonian memoirs."

Her tone bit like a rattlesnake, but all was not lost. She was gathering his wash, wasn't she? If things were beyond repair, she'd have left his laundry piled on the floor. "There's a roll of quarters in my—"

"I don't need anything from you."

"I'll meet you there in a few minutes, all right, Mol?"

"Don't bother." She opened the top dresser drawer and extracted the roll of quarters he'd mentioned.

He knew he was in the dog house. He had to offer a truce, but he couldn't help smiling. She was cute when she was mad. "Hey, Molly?"

Halfway out the door, she paused. "Yeah?"

"Give a holler if you can't work the machines, all right?"

"Shut up."

The door closed with a click behind her and his smile faded. What was he going to do? He couldn't stave her off forever, but she couldn't know the truth and love him better for it. And that was what he wanted, he realized. He wanted her to love him, despite the biggest mistake of his teenaged life—and the fact it had ended his mother's.

*   *   *

Brandywine, a glass of orange juice in her hand, slinked into a green ladder-back chair. She drummed her fingernails on the flour-dusted table. "I had a dream about Molly last night."

Star kneaded whole wheat dough at her breakfast table and raised her eyes to her daughter. Had Brandywine come into her own gift? "So did I."

"He's going to hurt her, isn't he?"

"Is that what your subconscious tells you?" Star covered the ball of dough with a gauzy towel and wiped her hands against her apron.

"I don't want this. I don't want to be able to do this."

If she didn't want it, perhaps her gift had found her at last. "How did your date go last night?"

"Fine. How the hell do you sleep at night, knowing the things you know?"

"I channel knowledge into good energy. You'll be able to do it, too, someday."

"What do I do until then? Sit around and watch this gorgeous, perfect man rip out Molly's heart? I know—somehow—he doesn't want to, but he can't help himself. Because deep inside he's a screaming child who needs to feed off her to survive."

"Don't be dramatic, Brandywine."

"You want to talk about drama? Picture Molly in a white hat. A frothy-looking thing with toile and a wide brim, and—"

"A black bow?"

"Yes. Looks like something out of 1910 high society in Europe."

Star took a seat. "That's your grandmother's hat."

"Where on earth would Grandma wear a hat like that?"

"To my knowledge, she never did wear it. But your aunts and I played dress-up as children."

"Whew." Brandywine relaxed against the chair back and sipped her juice. "I thought I was tapping a crazy well of auras and the unknown, but it turns out I'm only digging in my memories. Thank you, all gods."

"Thank them, indeed. They're helping you nurture your gift." Star swept the flour into a small pile on the table.

94

"I don't have a gift. It was just a dream."

"It was a bit more than that, dear. You've never seen that hat, nor have you seen pictures of it. We lost it in the move from the city to Parker's Landing, long before you were even a glimmer of hope in my mind. All that's left of that hat is the box in which it arrived on West Cullom Avenue in 1958."

*   *   *

Molly slung pillowcases stuffed with dirty laundry to the countertop in the hotel laundry facility, which steamed with visions of quick sex. Sex against the wall, sex atop the washing machine, and *eww,* sex on the folding counter. She gave it a once over. The incident had probably occurred ages ago. The hotel staff had hopefully cleaned since then.

But with so many visions permeating her brain, it was no wonder she couldn't decipher what had happened at Monticello that morning. She'd hit a nerve in asking about Scott's parents, but what choice did she have? The man was incapable of sharing. She'd *married* him, for God's sake. What more could she do to prove he could trust her?

Her cell phone vibrated against her hip. She pulled it from the waistband of her jazz pants, propped a leg atop the counter, and answered. "How do you always know when I need you?"

Brandywine's laugh resonated through the phone. "Since I call you all the time, odds are in my favor. So what's up?"

"His father's dead." Molly emptied the pillowcases onto the countertop and began to sort clothing into loads. "I don't know how long ago he died, or how, but it's a fresh sting."

"Ask about his mother."

"Oh, no. There's no way I'm mentioning his parents again. He flipped out, Brandy. Lost it. And now he's pretending nothing's wrong."

"So what? You're content with surface knowledge about cinnamon gum and satin sheets, and—"

"Who said anything about cinnamon gum?"

"You did."

"I don't think so, but thanks for reminding me." Molly reached for a pair of Scott's pants and searched the pockets for sticks of Big Red.

"He likes cinnamon gum, right? And satin sheets?"

"Yes on the gum, no on the sheets. He prefers flannel. What the hell is this?" Molly pulled a small, rectangular object from the pocket. Her brow furrowed when the image of Scott's hands grasping hers at the altar of Christ's Church overcame her. "A deck of cards." And she didn't need the eerie vision to remember how she'd come to be the ex-missus Scott Sheridan, thank you very much.

"What?"

"A tiny deck of playing cards, with Monticello on the backs. It's how he asked me to marry him."

"With Monticello cards? Honey, I've heard of tarot cards telling the future, and angel cards pointing the way, but how the hell do you propose with an ace of spades?"

"He said, 'Heart, we get married,' to be precise and then he drew one off the deck. Ten of hearts. We got married."

"All this time, we've had it wrong. We've been concentrating on *America Windows*, when we should have been focusing on that ridiculous proposal. You didn't have a chance at lasting with a beginning like that."

"I used to think it was charming." She fingered the worn rubber band securing the cards and flipped the item in her palm. "This might be the same deck."

"Hmm. You don't think he's going to propose again, do you?"

Molly shook her head and sighed. "How do you repeat a history so doomed?"

"Maybe he'll genuflect next time. Do you think he'll give you the same ring?"

"It doesn't matter because first of all, it isn't going to happen. And second, he wouldn't do it with a ring, or on one knee anyway."

"That's all right. Tradition is way over-rated."

Molly removed the rubber band and fanned through the deck, searching for the card that once paved the road of her future. "It's gone. No ten of hearts."

"Maybe he burned it."

The door creaked open, and Molly turned to see her ex-husband staring at her left hand. Or rather, at what she held in it.

*   *   *

Molly found the cards. He always kept their engagement card in his right rear pocket, to remind him of his vulnerability.

He swallowed hard and blinked into her gaze. "Hi."

"Brandy, I'll call you later." She snapped the cell phone shut. After a deep breath, she spoke. "I wasn't looking, or snooping, rather. I didn't mean to—"

"It's okay, cupcake." The words came out in a timid whisper, even as he boldly walked to within inches of her reach.

"Are these the same—"

"Yes." He held out his hand.

She pressed the deck into his palm. "You're missing our card."

"This one?" He reached behind her ear and produced the card in question.

"How did you—"

"Magic. I could tell you, but then I'd have to...do things to you. Good things, but things you might not want to do in a public laundry facility."

She turned back to her sorting. "This room was christened years ago."

"Is that right?"

With her subtle nod, a few stray auburn curls bounced against her shoulders, and his gaze traveled to the mounds of curls atop her head. "Why do you carry our cards around?"

"When I'm with you, I never know when I might have the urge to do something spontaneous."

"Such as?"

"Heart, you take your hair down." He fanned the deck in his hand and offered it to her.

With her arms elbows-deep in laundry, she looked up at him. Her breasts rose with a deep inhalation, and a breathy "Okay," accompanied her exhale. She selected a card. "Heart."

When she pulled the clip free, her hair cascaded down her back and settled against her shoulders in wild, tempting coils. "Heart, you tell me something personal," she countered.

He shrugged.

She pulled another card. Before she revealed it, her grin gave away the outcome. "Start talking."

"Something personal?"

"Raw and personal."

He took a step closer and slipped a hand into her curls. Wilkinson's description of "Jefferson red" was dead on, but that wasn't why he couldn't wait to bury his hands in his ex-wife's hair. "Molly." He met with the scent of lilac shampoo, and his cheek brushed against hers.

"Don't think this'll get you off the hook."

"You wanted personal." He rubbed his thumb along her cheekbone. "It doesn't get much more personal than this."

"This is physical, not p—"

He covered her mouth with his and their tongues met in a fervent exchange of heat and power. The air surrounding them peaked at least fifteen degrees within seconds. Lingering at her ear, and cupping a breast, he said, "Personal? I've imagined that kiss every day for the past five years. It's the kiss I should've given you back in Chicago, in front of the blue stained glass. And had I found the courage to do it, we wouldn't have lost five years because, believe me, no man leaves a woman he kisses like that."

"Heart, you take me to Port Royal."

A dull knife sliced him from the inside out. He ached to release the burden of what she longed to learn, but the lesson would surely taint any future they might have. Her hair, soft as spun silk, filtered between his fingers. "I want nothing more—"

"Tonight."

"—than to open my past to you, to make you part of it, to help you understand." His kiss melted on her neck. Her fingers tensed against his chest. He dropped the deck onto the counter.

She leaned into him, her breasts squashing against him. "I want to understand. Everything."

"And you will." Seeking her mouth, he lifted her to the countertop, and wedged himself between her legs. "Once we win the grant," he said, between kisses.

"Promise me."

"I promise. And I always keep my promises."

"As long as they don't end in 'I do.'"

"I intended to make good on that one, too. We all make mistakes. What do you say? Let me make it up to you?"

With a gasp, she tugged at the button on his jeans. "Second chance for you, professor."

"Should we…"

"Most definitely." Her fingers raked up the length of him.

His eyes closed amid the pleasure. He rolled his shoulders and felt the day's tension flee from his back. "I love what you do with your hands."

She caressed him from navel to chest and back again, with hands tunneled under his shirt, and massaged his neck with her lips.

"Oh, that mouth." He cupped her rear in both his hands, nudging her closer to his erection. He searched for a way inside her clothing, up her back and around her waist. *Great.* Today she wore one of those seamless, one-piece get-ups, layered with sweater-like pants rolled down at her hips. "Remind me to buy you some conventional clothes."

"These are more comfortable than conventional clothes."

Wasting no time, he slipped the leotard from her shoulders and inched it down her arms.

"This doesn't change things." She murmured at his lips and kicked off her clogs. "I'm still mad at you."

"You want me to tell you something even more personal to even the score?" He freed her arms from the leotard. "How about Wilkinson?"

She whisked his shirt from his body. "No need to discuss her at the moment."

"You accuse me of not talking about those close to me, but I told her all about you." He nipped at her earlobe and pressed tight to her torso, bare belly to bare belly. "I wouldn't have shut up about you if she'd gagged me."

"Scottie." She shoved his pants down and lifted her hips just enough to enable him to bare her.

"Talking about you—about us—kept us alive, and I wouldn't have let us die, if the world ended."

"Ever think of picking up the damn telephone?"

"Green Dockers," he whispered. "Right pocket."

"What?"

"Condom." He shoved her bra up and lowered his mouth to her breasts, as she blindly rifled through the pile of laundry.

Sweat broke between his shoulder blades, and a hazy mist of passion settled into his skin. Her breath—shallow, but intense with anticipation—feathered through his hair. Out of the corner of his eye, he spied a pair of olive green pants tangled in her hands.

"Got it," she said.

The pants landed in a heap at his feet, and the crinkling sound of a condom wrapper evoked a smile. No matter how many times he undressed her, the rush always rivaled that of the first time they'd been naked together, something akin to, *I can't believe I'm about to be inside this woman.*

Their gazes met as she unrolled the condom over him with patience. Every inch her fingers rubbed against him brought forth more pleasure, and when she finally reached the base of his cock, her fingers swept along the underside of his balls.

His urgent need for her couldn't wait another second. He parted her labia with his thumbs and plunged his shaft into her hot, wet abyss.

"Good Lord," he whispered, pumping in and out.

She was tight and quivering, gripping his shoulders, digging her fingernails into his flesh. "Don't stop." Her words escaped, gruff and certain.

"Never." He pulled her from the counter and twirled toward a washing machine half-full with his socks and boxer shorts. He spun her on his cock—he had to take her from behind—and she caught the top of the appliance for balance.

The curves of her hips made decent grab-bars. He physically moved her over his cock and banged her ass against his lower abdomen over and over again. Her delightful cries became muffled when he offered her a finger to suck.

He shoved into her channel one last time before dialing things down a notch. "I don't know why I can't be gentle with you." He lifted her leg by its muscular thigh, and again turned her, as if his shaft were a barbecue spit, and she, his hunted dinner. When she pulled her lips off his finger, his cock twitched against her insides.

"You're gentle with me"—she locked her legs around his waist— "when it's time to be gentle. But when it's time to have it out—"

His kiss silenced her. He lifted her, swung her around, and thrust into her as her back met the cement-block wall opposite the folding counter. Bracing against the wall, he achieved the full depth of her vagina. "Oh, Molly."

She licked the inside of his mouth, dragged her tongue along the underside of his.

His dewy sweat turned to heavy beads—damn, it was hot in here— and each time his pelvis pressed up to hers, their flesh melded, only to peel apart with his next withdrawal.

"Ohhh," she groaned against his mouth. "Baby, I—"

"I love you, too." He came with a gushing release and swept his tongue against hers. "I love you, too."

Her breasts heaved as she struggled to catch her breath, and her damp cheek pressed against his. "I wasn't going to say that."

He lowered her feet to the floor, and the proverbial knife appeared on the inside of his stomach again. He'd been certain she was about to confess her feelings. Why else would she have called him "baby"? It was an emotional trigger, he realized. Because she'd used the endearment five years ago every time she'd told him she loved him, he'd expected to hear it now. And what had possessed him to tell her something he was only eighty percent sure of? Well, maybe ninety,

ninety-five, but still... *Idiot.*

She smiled, struggling for an even breath, and tossed her hair over a shoulder. "But that's what I call personal, all right." Her arm brushed against his moist chest when she crossed the room.

As he peeled the condom from his softening penis, his thumb caught in the latex and ripped it. Or had it torn before? He investigated. The tear was on the underside, near the head. The past few minutes *had* been rather uninhibited. But had the sex been rough enough to destroy a condom?

He discarded the semen-drenched prophylactic and looked toward Molly. If he'd come inside her, his fluid would drip between her thighs, but she'd whisked one of his shirts around her body, thereby covering the area in question.

She'd often tossed on his clothes after sex, and her doing so now evoked warm memories—memories of a comfortable coupling, of a strong bond, unbreakable. Or so he'd thought until the moment she set foot inside the drawing room at Shirley Plantation during their historical homes tour.

There's an angry presence here, Scottie. Who's Aunt Pratt?

He'd known they were over the second she'd explained her family's eerie talents. Forever had suddenly become a lot shorter.

He turned to gather the cards, which were strewn about the room. "I do, you know. Love you."

"I don't see what good that does either of us." She piled the machine full of clothing and placed quarters into the slot. "Whether or not you loved me was never a question in my mind."

"Good, because I—"

"It was your leaving that shocked the hell out of me." She pushed the lever in to start the water, but nothing happened. She pushed it in again and again, to no avail. "Damn it."

He pocketed the special deck of cards, and before he withdrew his hand, he fingered the wedding ring pinned in the pocket lining.

'Damn it' was right. He'd have to take her to Port Royal. It was either that or say goodbye. And he'd barely survived that the first time around.

He leaned over her, readjusted the quarters, and heard the *cha-ching* as the fare registered. Water rushed in the machine; ambivalence, through his heart.

CHAPTER 9

One week later, at daybreak, Scott awoke amid tremors and sweat. Not in a good way, but with visions of his mother's beautiful, lifeless body in a pool of blood. Good Lord, he'd discovered the crime scene. Did he have to dream about it for the rest of his life?

He rolled toward Molly. The sight of her calmed his nerves, and once his hands stopped shaking, he ran his fingers through her hair—an unusual, shimmering shade of copperish auburn.

Sally Hemings had given birth to several red-headed children. Thomas Jefferson may have awaited news of healthy babies, even though laws against miscegenation prohibited him acknowledging them as his own. *What a terrible dilemma.*

Scott caressed his ex-wife from her cheekbone to her chin. So intriguing, so naturally gorgeous, so very briefly his. And now that he had her back in his life, he couldn't lose her again. If Molly were to give birth to his children, would he allow the barriers of his past to stand in the way?

Never. It's time to return to Honey Hill.

*   *   *

Molly awoke to a persistent knocking on the door. She kicked toward her ex-husband, who should've answered it by now, only her feet never reached him. She lifted her head from the too-soft pillows and parted the frizzy jungle her hair had become overnight.

Scott wasn't in bed. A quick glance out the sliding glass door told her he wasn't breakfasting on the balcony, as he'd often done. Just like Jefferson, he savored the moment the sun rose, watched every moment of it. Occasionally made love to her while the sun brightened the sky, too. Had Jefferson ever pleasured Sally Hemings at dawn?

The knocking continued.

Molly blew a curl off her forehead and pulled her naked body from the bed. "Scottie?"

"Mrs. Sheridan?" An unfamiliar male voice.

Molly squinted through sleep-filled eyes at the clock—8:02—and sighed when she realized she'd overslept. No time for a morning jog today.

"I'm sorry to wake you. My name is Travis Brown. I'm a student of your husband's."

"My husband, er Scott, doesn't appear to be here." She threw on one of his shirts and hurried to the bathroom.

"The professor said you'd need a ride to the library this morning, Mrs. Sheridan."

"Um, you can call me Molly, and"—she quickly scanned the room for signs of her ex-husband. But he was nowhere to be seen—and her car keys weren't in their usual location atop the desk—"and, if you don't mind my asking, do you know where Dr. Sheridan might be?"

"He said he'd left you a note, ma'am. He had some family business to take care of, but he'll meet us at Monticello by lunchtime."

"Lunch?"

"That's what he said."

"I, uh, okay. Thanks for coming for me."

"Yes, ma'am. He said you'd be ready at eight, but if you need some time, perhaps I can—"

"Just a few minutes."

"If you'd prefer, I can make a donut run while you're getting ready. Are you hungry?"

"I don't eat breakfast, but thank you anyway. I'll be ready in a few minutes." She pulled the scale out from beneath the vanity and stepped onto it.

"I'm parked right outside, Mrs. Sheridan. I have a blue Jetta with rust on the driver side door."

"Thank you, Travis." She looked down with caution at the scale, only to find Scott had stuck a Post-it note over the numbers.

"Cupcake," she read, "handling family business. Thinking of your third orgasm. Wow."

Family business, pshaw. She'd come to feel jealous at the mention of anything related to his unknown family, and if he really had family business to tend to, why couldn't he have enlisted her help?

Her first instinct was to crumble the note and toss it in the trash, but, on second thought, she smoothed it. The memento would make a nice addition to her Scott Sheridan collection, presently housed in a black-and-white striped hatbox—currently missing—in her attic.

She once again looked to the scale. *One hundred nineteen pounds. Ouch! To Do List: Boast weight gain to Aunt Star and then cry behind closed doors.*

She'd have a good cry now, if she had time to wallow. She squeezed the skin at her hips. *Fat.* Although Scott found her love handles convenient during backwards sex—and wasn't shy about telling her so—she wished she had time to find a ballet studio, rent some floor time, and spend a good hour stretching at the *barre.* She twisted her rear toward the mirror and glanced over her shoulder at her reflection. "I miss dance class."

*   *   *

Leaning against the hood of Molly's car—he enjoyed sharing things with her again—Scott shaded his eyes from the hot morning sun and looked up at Honey Hill.

He'd grown up here—far too quickly. The ghosts in the large, red-brick house taunted him enough to send him down the road with tires squealing. But when he closed his eyes and took a deep breath of river-scented air, memories of the home he preferred to remember—the home he'd known before the beatings—propelled him back toward the gate.

No Sheridan had set foot on the property for years, but, with the exception of the faded sign at the foot of the drive, the empty house looked anything but abandoned. The lawn appeared as well-groomed as it had been in its heyday, reflecting diamond-shapes, like on a baseball outfield, and the shutters and trim gleamed with fresh evergreen paint.

The family's estate fund covered the constant upkeep of the house, allowing Scott to maintain a safe distance. Renee and Hannah wanted to sell the place before the money was depleted, but he couldn't bring himself to put the land on the market. Too much history.

The home had been in his mother's family for generations. Someday—maybe today—he hoped to face the demons beyond that front door and make the house a home again. If not his home, a place for one of his sisters. Perhaps for Renee, who was pregnant with child number five and hoping for her first girl.

Then again, were he and his siblings capable of living in a structure concealing memories of spousal abuse? Of murder and suicide? Such a waste. His mother's legacy *and* his parents' lives.

He opened the gate and hitched the iron door so the wind wouldn't blow it closed, just as he'd done the day he'd found his parents' lifeless bodies in the southwest wing. It felt like only yesterday, the sting fresh. Over the years, the anxiety had only waned for a month here and there. He'd often awakened, as he had this morning, with visions of the horrid scene dancing in his head. It would never end. It would always be part of him.

Molly's wedding ring in his pocket provided psychological support as he inched toward the double doors.

Time to open them.

He licked his dry lips with a cottony tongue.

Pull yourself together.

A lump formed in his throat when he inserted the key.

This place is yours for the taking. Your birthright. Manifest Destiny. Be a man. Take it.

The door creaked open, and the scent of aged wood and moth balls drifted out to the portico. He peaked into the vestibule, where a baby grand piano still sat, covered with a grey tarp. Hannah had wanted to keep the instrument, but for lack of anywhere to store it, she opted to keep where it had always been. She'd thought she'd come for it at a later date, but she had her own piano now, one without terrifying memories.

If he closed his eyes, he imagined the music his mother and sisters would play on holidays. He nearly smiled, before he remembered those celebrations had often ended with Ellie Sue's bruised flesh, and—on the one occasion in which he'd stepped between them—his own.

By age seven, he'd realized the fiery nature of his father's temper far surpassed the norm. He'd been a coward not to interfere, regardless of Nathaniel's power with the horse whip. Near the end, he could have held his own, rivaling his old man. Although he chose to keep his distance, he'd certainly played his part in the final tragedy.

During a day trip to Washington, D. C., the Memorial Day weekend before his parents' death, he'd purchased an illegal revolver and the six rounds of ammunition it held. "Point it and shoot," he told his mother. "You have the right to bear arms against your enemy."

While he expected Nathaniel to give her reason, he never dreamed Ellie Sue would squeeze the trigger. Scott had believed a gun would scare the bite out of the beast, so to speak. By July fourth, he realized he'd never been more wrong. Nothing—not even leaving Molly in tears at the Art Institute of Chicago—came close to that misjudgment.

With a held breath, he stepped onto the walnut planks past the threshold. His footfalls echoed throughout the vast house, and his arms turned to gooseflesh, despite the oppressive heat within.

On what would have been his and Molly's first anniversary, he'd managed to open the door and peer inside, but he hadn't been this deep in the entrails of the building since the week following the funeral.

Like the main house at Tuckahoe Plantation, the Sheridan family mansion was H-shaped. The formal rooms, those off the east or "carriage" entrance, were easy to tour, for it was there his parents and ancestors had entertained guests. Nothing out of place there, with nary a fist swinging for public viewing in the front parlors.

But the west wing represented reality. Far out of earshot was the master suite, where, over the years, Nathaniel's rage had often overcome Ellie Sue's fragile body. It was the room Scott would investigate today, if he could muster the courage.

The main staircase ascended just west of the entrance, in the connecting part of the "H." With a tentative gait, he climbed. One step at a time, his hand trembling along the cherry banister, removing a trail of dust along the way.

Housekeeping tended to the place quarterly, and considering that, the place was in reasonably good shape. However, Honey Hill deserved to look as it did in its prime—like a proud resort along the Rappahannock.

He remembered spring cleaning, when his mother and sisters had opened all windows and buckled down until the place gleamed. Everything from Sunday silver to the crystal chandelier in the dining room received a brisk polishing. The scent of flax soap and fresh Virginia air filtered through his memory.

He'd never lent a hand; indoor chores, from the day his forefathers had erected the plantation, were women's work. His tasks involved horse stables and storm windows.

A chill darted up his spine as the memories faded and he found himself standing on the second floor landing, facing the closed door leading to the master suite. Sweat beaded at his temples—it was ungodly warm in the house—and his heart raced. He pinched his eyes shut, but couldn't sweep away the recollection of what he'd found beyond that door.

Now or never. He traversed the hallway and reached for the doorknob. When he twisted it, the door stuck. "You've got to be kidding me."

He pushed again and rattled the knob, with no luck. He slapped the heel of his hand against the door's upper corners, but the swollen wood didn't budge. Didn't it just figure. He'd come this far—actually touched the door—and for nothing. "Thanks for nothing, Gracie."

And now he blamed scientifically-explained expansion of wood in a humid climate on a ghost in Parker's Landing, Illinois. He'd lost his mind.

He thudded his forehead against the door.

The door popped open.

*   *   *

"Where's our guy?"

Molly looked up from the Louis XV silver vase displayed on her computer screen. Wilkinson peered over the top of Molly's study cube at UVA's library, sporting a grin.

Molly stuck a pencil into her bun and silently cursed her over-sleeping, which had left her with barely enough time for a quick rinse in the shower, let alone a good scrubbing of her hair. The only solace had been no overlap in her schedule with the University of Virginia's. If she had to look like hell, at least it wouldn't be for her rival's viewing—or so she'd thought.

She painted on a smile. "Good morning, Professor Wilkinson."

"It's *Doctor* Wilkinson actually. Is that an original Louis XV?"

"My apologies, and yes." Molly blinked back to her computer screen and jotted some specifics onto her notepad. "Wasting your time here at the library while your team has free rein of Monticello?"

"The big house is in good hands, I assure you."

"As is Dr. Sheridan." No news was good news after all. And she hadn't heard "boo" from him since three in the morning, when he'd lost a hand in her hair. Warm pleasure darted between her thighs as she recalled the events leading up to that moment.

"Glad to hear."

"Now, may I help you with something?"

Wilkinson flared her fingers and focused on her nails. "It's something I should discuss with Scott."

107

"I'll have him call."

"I don't wait around for the phone to ring. That's the difference between us."

"Beg your—"

"Mrs. Sheridan?" Travis popped up on the other side of the cube. "I have the specifics on the accessories you requested, but there's still no word on the *tête à tête*."

"Thanks." *For calling me missus at just the right time.*

"Having trouble tracking down a few pieces?" Wilkinson peered at the computer screen. "I hope you'll have them by presentation time."

"We should get moving, ma'am," Travis piped up. "I promised your husband I'd have you in the gardens by noon."

"Yes, thanks." Molly gathered her papers. Wilkinson's stare beat down on the back of her head like a beam through a magnifying glass. If she were an ant on the sidewalk, she'd have fried by now, and Wilkinson wasn't relenting. "May I help you?" Molly met her gaze.

"Let me guess." Wilkinson's eyes narrowed. "He's detained by mysterious family business?"

"Yes, as a matter of fact." Molly looked over the other side of the cube to where Travis filed his notes, seemingly uninterested.

"I'll bet you'd kill for a glimpse of said business." Wilkinson spoke just above a whisper. "But your ex-husband's tight-lipped when it comes to Honey Hill."

"Honey-what?"

"Honey Hill. I'm willing to fill you in." Wilkinson again looked at the vase on the computer screen. "For whatever you have on the Louis. What do you say? Make this race even more interesting? You win, you keep Scott and whatever you find at Honey Hill. I win, I keep my position here at UVA and the Louis XV on display in the Dome Room."

*   *   *

Scott lifted his head. The looming space before him was a grotto of gruesome memories, but, at a glance, it was nothing more than hardwood and plaster. The interior shutters prohibited the sunlight from brightening the room, but fifteen years ago, it had been a vivid space filled with sunshine.

He looked to the corner near the window, where an armoire had once stood, where his mother had taken her own life. And suddenly, they were there again.

His father's blood was splattered against the far wall, his body rumpled at the foot of the window. He looked like horror; she remained beautiful. Her usually golden hair was red with blood, but her face, white as a sheet, wore a pleasant expression, as if an amusing dream played on the backs of her eyelids.

Vomit and grief rose in his throat, and he turned toward the hallway. Once outside the room, the nausea relented; the grief, however, stuck with him.

*   *   *

Star loaded green canisters and cookie jars into the kiln, but her mind was nowhere near her pottery. Molly's ex-husband, portraying self-deprecation and -destruction, occupied her every thought.

His nightmares had begun to eat into his daytime. The scene in his mind replayed time and time again because he continually missed an important detail. *But what?* He'd better figure it out soon, or Molly's blue might never dissipate.

*   *   *

Honey Hill. According to Wilkinson, Scott carried a key that unlocked the door, although he rarely visited the plantation and never brought company.

If Molly wanted answers, she'd have to take a drive out to Port Royal herself, find the Sheridan estate, and enter at her own risk. The task would be nearly impossible. Wilkinson wouldn't say where in Port Royal Honey Hill stood, and chances of her skimming his keys from him were slim to nil.

Scott's ex-trollop hadn't given Molly much information in exchange for an original Louis XV vase available for loan, and Scott would probably blow a gasket when he learned of their recent deal. But what choice did Molly have?

If Scott Sheridan was going to claim her—again—she sure as hell would know the whole story before handing over what little of her heart she'd yet to give him.

CHAPTER 10

Tomorrow afternoon was do or die. After four-and-a-half weeks of research, it was finally time to present to the curator, and they were down to the wire to find an original *tête à tête*.

Scott spun Molly's wedding ring around the tip of his little finger. Lord, she'd worn it well. Ironic that the two reasons he'd run from her—Jeffersonian history and her inexplicable talent to "feel" what had transpired in a room when entering it—now brought them back together.

Perhaps she was correct in assuming every step along the way led to a predetermined destiny. How else would they have come so far? They'd spent more consecutive nights together now than when they were married, and while they'd been meticulous with birth control, it had failed in the laundry facilities a few weeks back.

A frightening suspicion that fate might actually work in mysterious ways haunted him. And if they were meant to be together? Well, he had some explaining to do along the guided tour of Honey Hill.

Maybe she could accept the role he'd played in his mother's death as a stepping stone along his path. Was it too late to consider making good on his promise? He might invite her out to Port Royal and give it a whirl, but he couldn't consider that now. And frankly, neither could she.

"After the presentation," he whispered to himself. "One thing at a time."

Hearing the click of her key in the lock and a "Damn it, Gracie," when the door didn't open, he slipped her ring into the pocket of his shirt and met her at the threshold. "How was your day, cupcake?"

"Productive." With a pink glow in her cheeks and her hair bouncing against her back and shoulders, she rustled past him carrying six shopping bags from various stores, hung two plastic-clad hangers on the rod, and dropped the rest of her wares on the bed.

"Sounds promising." He slouched back into the lone chair and tapped the eraser end of a pencil against a legal pad. "What did you find?"

She planted a kiss hard and center on his mouth.

"Mmm, I love it when you shop." He abandoned the pencil and wove his hands into her wild hair. "It puts you in a mood fit for—"

"We're going to win this thing." She threw a leg over his lap and straddled him on the spot.

He groaned. "A mood fit for this." He rubbed her from knee to hip. "What did you buy?"

"Rice cakes," she said between kisses and ground her pelvis against his.

The great thing about dancewear: he could feel all of her through the thin material. The bummer about it: it was nearly impossible to undress her gracefully, which was what he almost always wanted to do.

"Six bags of rice cakes?"

"And a little black dress to wear tomorrow—"

"I love little clothes, leaves plenty to my advantage."

"—and a blazer to wear over it."

"Hmm." He caressed her from hip to knee and back again. "No need to hide this body, so burn it."

"A book about channeling energy for Aunt Star…and a snazzy little number for the cocktail hour tonight."

"Can't wait to see it."

"I hope it fits. I didn't have time to try it on."

"By any chance, did you buy a pregnancy test?"

She cupped his face in her hands and propped her leg on his shoulder. "Tell me we have the *tête à tête*."

"They were unwilling to sell—"

"Everyone has a price."

"But with the appropriate amount of persuasion…" He tucked a few fingers into the scoop neck of her leotard and trailed his pinky over the satiny brassiere. "Let's just say 'goal accomplished.'"

"Oh, thank goodness. What color upholstery? It's original, I hope?"

"I don't have the slightest idea."

"You didn't ask?"

"I wrote it down, but I'm too busy wondering what you've got on under this thing."

"Let me see your notes." She twisted on his lap, which only pressed her most intimate parts closer to his.

His hand found a new home and briskly massaged her. "Lord, Miss Molly, no woman should have the right to bend this way." He pressed her hips to his torso and imagined a slow penetration into her strong, wet depths. But they didn't have time for recreation. They were due at Michie Tavern in less than an hour.

"A violet brocade. Is that what she said?"

"Is that what I wrote?"

"No, but I think it's what you meant to write."

He scooped her up and deposited her onto the bed, next to her purchases. "Very well then, a violet brocade." He leaned into a kiss. "Let's see this dress."

When she smiled in a playful way, her nose wrinkled.

"And do me a favor." He brushed another kiss over her lips. "Show off the freckles tonight. They drive me crazy."

"They drive me insane." She grabbed a black garment bag, scrambled up and hooked the hanger onto the closet rod before she made her way to the bathroom.

The door closed and, within seconds, he heard the familiar sound of metal sliding against the tile floor. "Get off that damn scale."

"Oh, my God." Her whisper carried a tremor of fear.

"Molly?"

"Oh, my God."

He rapped on the door. "Let me in."

"I'm fat."

"I had you naked at daybreak. You're not fat." He opened the door a sliver to see her scrambling out of her one-piece leotard. She stepped back onto the scale, nude, stared down at the numbers, and shook her head. He pushed the door wide open. "Get off the scale."

She blinked up at him, tears welling on her lashes. "I'm up another three pounds."

"You look great."

She looked back to the numbers. "I don't look great. I look one-twenty-two."

"Then one-twenty-two is phenomenal."

"That's twelve extra pounds. Twelve pounds in a month."

"Maybe you needed it."

"I didn't need chocolate, Scottie. I didn't need ice cream and Oreos and—"

"You don't eat much of any of those things."

"Over the past few weeks, I haven't been able to stop."

"Once or twice a week means 'haven't been able to stop'? Don't be ridiculous."

"The scale doesn't lie."

Well, it could. He'd wheel it back a few pounds as soon as she fell asleep. "Maybe you're pregnant."

"I told you before." She shook her head, stepped off the scale, and shouldered past him. "I'm not pregnant."

"We've been holed up in this tiny cell of a room for a month now, and—"

"Who's fault is that? We could've ventured out to Honey Hill."

"And I've yet to see a tampon wrapper, first of all. And secondly, Port Royal is hours away."

"I'm not pregnant."

"I grew up with two sisters, Molly. I know how things work."

"Two sisters?" With shaking legs, she climbed between the sheets. "And stop looking at me."

"Yes, two sisters, and I'm looking at you because I haven't been able to stop looking at you in weeks."

"In order to be pregnant, I'd have to ovulate, and I don't do that."

"Maybe you do now." He sat next to her and combed a curl behind her ear. "I'll go get a test."

"No." She closed her hand tightly over his. "Do you know what a fluke that would be? I haven't ovulated in four-and-a-half years. It's a side effect."

"Of what?"

"Low body fat percentage."

"About that." He sighed. "Are you all right? You seem to be—"

"I'm fine."

"You're obsessed with your weight."

"I'm not obsessed. I'm careful."

"I don't like this, Molly, this craziness. You let the numbers on that scale depict your self-worth, and I don't like it."

"You're one to talk about my self-worth. Are you forgetting what you did to me at *America Windows*?"

"I wish we both could forget. I—"

"There I was, lulled by the rain—and the hand you'd strategically placed on my back—staring up at a chorus line, smiling children, and moons galore, and bam. Divorce. If you thought I was something worth holding onto, do you think we'd be here now? Discussing my one-hundred-and-twenty-two pounds of flabby thighs, which haven't seen the likes of a dance floor since you dragged me here?"

"I won't acknowledge something so ludicrous."

"You won't acknowledge a damn thing."

"I'm acknowledging my responsibility, should you happen to be carrying my child someday."

"It won't happen. I don't work that way."

"Maybe the gods of fate will try to tell you something."

"Stop saying things you don't mean and avert your eyes, so I can stuff this fat ass into a cocktail dress."

He draped a curl behind her ear. "You're a beautiful woman, Molly. I'm sorry you question your worth because of my mistake at *America Windows*. I promise—I'll make it up to you, and you will understand someday. Now get dressed."

With a frown, she stomped to the closet. He watched her wiggle her now-healthy-looking body into a pair of panties. She pulled a floor-length, purplish blue dress from the garment bag.

He stepped in beside her and pulled a suit from the closet.

"Excuse me." She carried the dress to the bathroom and disappeared behind the door.

"Stay off the scale." He dressed in silence. When he discreetly pinned her wedding ring to the lining of his sports coat, he heard her whimpering. "Molly?"

"It doesn't fit." She appeared with tearing eyes in an open-zippered gown. "It doesn't fit."

"Maybe you should have tried it on."

"It's a six, and I'm always a six."

"Maybe now you're a seven."

"If I could be a seven, I'd gladly be a seven, but dress sizes go by even numbers, and I cannot—absolutely cannot—be an eight. That's like going from twenty-eight to thirty in one year. Skipping twenty-nine."

"Cupcake, I went from *eighteen* to forty, and I don't want to hear it. You look great. Start feeling great because we're short on time." He took a step toward her.

"Go without me."

"Do you think I'd do that when you're the brains behind this entire operation? Not a chance." He turned her around and yanked on the material. "Suck in, and I'll zip it up."

"Suck in?"

"I grew up with two sisters, so I know how this is done. Suck in."

She inhaled sharply, and he swept the zipper up her back. "Doesn't fit, huh? Looks good from where I'm standing." He patted her on the rear. "Remember. Show off the freckles."

"Dresses aren't usually this tight on me. I doubt I'll make it through one course of southern food." She reached for a bag of rice cakes. "Better eat some air."

"The faire at Michie Tavern is as legendary as its original patrons." He straightened his tie. "I don't know why you're filling up on those things."

"I'll give you one hundred-twenty-two reasons."

"Stop."

"I haven't been over one-fifteen ever, and I prefer to stay at one-ten."

"Come here." He tugged her by the elbow to the full-length mirror. "Why do you pay attention to the numbers when you look like this?"

She folded her arms over her midsection and refused to look directly at her reflection.

"Humor me, Miss Molly."

"Listen, I may not be fat by average standards, but this is the way it starts, a pound here, a pound—"

"Drop your arms."

"You've seen Dusky, right? The rest of us are the same. We buried my grandmother at one-hundred-eighty-two pounds. My mother: Oompa Loompa. Aunt Star: A taller version of my mother. And Brandy's still young, but if she isn't careful, she'll—"

"I said, drop your arms."

She tapped her toes, pursed her lips, and refused.

"Take a good, hard look." He raked through her long, full hair and nodded toward the mirror. "You're not the only one hoping to end vicious cycles your forefathers set in motion, so get over it." He pulled her tight to his body, then turned her and laid a kiss on her mouth. "And do it fast because we've got a schedule to keep."

*   *   *

One hundred-twenty-two pounds. And she must be fat if Scott thought she was pregnant. He opened the door for her at Michie Tavern, and she entered the ancient establishment. It figured Wilkinson would wear something conservative and basic black, but how she managed to look like a funeral director and ooze with sex appeal at the same time was beyond Molly. *To Do List: Spill a drink in Wilkinson's lap. Knock her down a few pegs.*

"Come on, cupcake. You look great." His drawl seemed thicker than usual, but she wasn't going to fall for that old trick again.

Members of the Thomas Jefferson Foundation welcomed them to the benefit, and she painted on her best smile, inhaling the aromas of Southern cuisine. Still, through it all, the faint scent of cinnamon gum—always the scent of Scott—lingered in the air. So good, so comforting. Too bad it would all end tomorrow if the foundation awarded the grant to the University of Virginia.

A tickle raced up her back and hairs on her arm stood on end. The man would always send a surge up her spine with a touch.

But...

She looked up at him to make sure.

He hadn't touched her this time. He was shaking hands with a board member and fiddling with the inside liner of his jacket. And there it was again. A tingling sensation darted from the small of her back to the nape of her neck, like a cool breeze. It *was* rather windy tonight, but it was a balmy, whispering wind, hardly the type to chill.

Her cheeks felt numb, her throat, dry, and suddenly, a rash of heat swept over her. A hot flash maybe? But as screwed up as she was in the menstrual sense, she refused to believe she was menopausal. And regardless of what Scott had said, there was no way she'd conceived. Condoms and not even a slim chance she'd ovulated disproved that theory in a blink.

Perhaps she was coming down with a flu bug, although she wouldn't feel the least bit ill, if she ignored the black spot suddenly clouding her vision. "Scottie," she whispered, grasping his hand.

She focused on his shamrock green eyes.

"Molly?" He squeezed her hand. "Are you all right?"

She swallowed hard and nodded. "Someone died here."

A smile shot across his face like a star through the sky. "Well, of course someone died here. This building dates back to the 1700s. Couple a tavern with the right to bear arms and—"

"I don't think you understand. I'm feeling it."

* * *

It came as no surprise to him that she'd felt the death lingering in the walls of the old establishment, but he'd never known it to affect her physically. He licked his lips and pulled an auburn sprig of hair from her suddenly pale forehead. "Are you sure?"

She shook her head. "We have the *tête à tête*, right?"

"What? I don't care about that weird chair, Molly, I—"

"Take me to the Dome Room." She nibbled on her lower lip and knit her brow. "Now, while I'm cooking. This could be our last chance before the presentations. I might feel something."

He nodded, and without so much as excusing himself from the company of the TJF, he grasped her under the elbow and whisked her out the door, each of them scurrying through the parking lot, rushing to reach Monticello's gates before sundown.

When they arrived, the last of the tourists were meandering out the plantation doors. Scott flashed his Washington and Lee ID at the docent at the East entrance. "We have to get into the Dome Room."

"You have about twenty minutes."

"That's all we need," Molly said. An active pink tinted her cheeks, and her hair had begun to frizz. "Just a few minutes."

He squeezed her hand and led her up to the third floor.

She rushed across the wooden floor and paused dead center in the Dome Room. Her posture was straight, the heel of her right foot positioned at the arch of her left in some dancer's stance. With her face lifted heavenward, and the setting sun blazing orange through the west windows, she appeared almost angelic. But the slant of her mouth, the slight shake of her head, depicted graceful regret.

He fingered the lining of his jacket and stole a feel of the sapphire ring pinned there. Talk about regret. "Molly, I—"

"Shh." She raised her hand like a traffic cop and lowered it with a fluid motion reminiscent of those he'd seen on the dance floor back in Parker's Landing. "There's passion here. You can't deny it."

He gave a quick nod.

"Passion between a man and his home, pride in his workmanship and design. Pain for what lay in waste. Do you think he enjoyed life here at Monticello?"

"I think he intended to."

"But life got in the way, is that what you think? Do you think he was a happy man?"

"Do you think he wasn't?"

"I don't know what I think anymore." She slipped her foot from a strappy, silver high-heeled sandal and brushed her toe against the aged wood upon which she stood. "But the magic of this place, its beauty, its intrigue... One of the most influential men this country has ever seen walked these floors. He had high hopes for us, didn't he? He wanted for us what he never had."

"Politically speaking, I think he took great pride in all he accomplished."

"But there is no mention of politics in his epitaph. This was his passion. Family, home. He surrounded himself with lovely things, lovely books, lovely people. All an escape, all fillers for what he couldn't acknowledge. For whom he couldn't recognize. Sally. Their children."

"I don't think of it that way. I prefer—"

"Of course. You're the same man."

Pride rushed in with his next breath, but... "Somehow I don't think you meant that as a compliment."

"Some say Jefferson was an easy man to know, friendly. But they also say knowing him well was an impossible feat. How well do I know you, Dr. Sheridan?"

"You know me."

"You're the most intelligent man I've ever shared a conversation with, and you loved me, Scottie—don't you dare tell me otherwise—but the fact you can stand there, forcing commitment only if I happen to be pregnant with your child... It's insulting."

He caught his jaw before it clanged to the floor, and not knowing what else to do, he caressed the special jewel he'd hidden in his coat and approached her. "I'm not afraid to commit. Six days and a ring on your finger proved that years ago."

"Oh, you can commit. It's honoring your commitments that troubles you. Unless, of course, you're legally bound with a Jeffersonesque red-headed baby."

"That's not what I meant earlier. What I meant was..." Not three inches of air filtered between them, and he wrapped his arms around her in a nearly forceful embrace, pulling her tight to his body. "Wouldn't it be easier if fate decided this for us? If I didn't have to worry about whether you could accept all there is to see in me? If you didn't have to worry about twelve damned pounds?"

She dragged her fingers over his chest in calming strokes, but blinked up at him with a hard gaze. "You appall me, professor," she

118

whispered.

Their mouths met not an instant later, and before they came up for air, he'd backed her against the west window, where the setting sun raced through her auburn curls, brightening them to a fiery red. His fingers gathered periwinkle silk, inching it up her supple thighs.

"By the way"—her voice was a mixture of passion and heat; it had never sounded more sexual—"the *tête à tête* isn't weird. It's a genius piece of distinctive furniture. A lovers' chair, designed for the interaction of couples, for the enrichment of shared knowledge. Not that I expect you to understand the concept of emotional coupling in any capacity."

"I understand." He tucked a thumb under the barely-there thong nestled between her scrumptious cheeks and followed it to her moist opening. "In more capacities than you realize. Right rear pocket."

"Condom?" She reached into the pocket and extracted the ten of hearts.

"No condom. I didn't plan on shagging you before sunset."

"Shagging me? Who says you're getting anywhere?" In a mad scramble, she dropped the card, yanked on the buckle of his belt and slipped a hand into his pants. "What could have possibly given you the impression we'd—"

"Lord, how I missed those hands."

*   *   *

His groan—and the hard cock in her hand—sprang her back to reality. For a moment, she'd forgotten where they were and what they were about to do. "I have no self-control when I'm with you."

"That makes two of us." He nuzzled her neck and breathed into her ear when she gave him another long, slow stroke and shoved his pants down his hips. A pack of cinnamon chewing gum slapped against the wooden planks.

Everyone who'd gained access to the third floor of Monticello was presently milling about Michie Tavern. The Dome Room was at their private disposal. He cupped her rear, threatened to penetrate her with his fingers.

"You know me, Molly. You've always known me. Better than anyone."

"In that case, not a soul has touched you." She ripped the jacket from his shoulders and sent it sailing halfway across the room. It settled, buttons clinking against the floor, beneath the oculus. "And I'd say my initial analysis of this room was accurate enough."

"Dead-on." He toyed with the string of her thong, while trailing the other hand under her thigh, raising her leg. Once again in a vertical split against him, she managed to exhale a shuddering breath as he held her against the mirrored glass of the circular window and whispered against her lips, "Molly Catherine."

"We're going to win tomorrow," she whispered back.

He rubbed his nose against hers, his penis twitching at the apex of her legs. "I love a confident woman." His hot mouth worked magic against her neck, his tongue dragging against her flesh, taunting her.

She tightened her arms around him, wound her fingers into his black hair. "No god would be so cruel as to take you from me twice."

"Do you love me?" He pulled her panties aside. "Enough to stay if we lose?"

"I think the question is whether you love me enough not to leave."

"Lord, Molly." With tiny jabs, the tip of his cock teased its way inside her. "I'd follow half your smile for thousands of miles." He drove into her with one last, thorough plunge, which darted pleasure from her depths to the tips of her elevated toes.

"Oh, Scottie."

He traced her lip line with his tongue, silencing her, and with his hands squeezing against her rear, he drew her hips closer to meet his next thrust.

Lost in ecstasy, she rested her head against the window, as he slowly manipulated and occupied her body. He filled her patiently and precisely, as if oblivious to their present location, as if he'd made love to her fifty times against this wall. As if getting caught wouldn't immediately dash any chance for his university to receive the grant of a lifetime.

She snapped her eyes open; he instantly met her gaze and mumbled against her lips, "You know me." He ground deeper into her body, his lashes fluttering against her cheek. He touched her softly on the chin. "Miss Molly."

"Mmm-hmm?"

He penetrated in slow, even strokes, tantalizing her from the inside out, pulling her closer and closer to heaven. "Love you," he breathed.

"I love you, too."

*   *   *

He'd kissed all the lipstick from her lips, but climbing the steps at

Michie Tavern, she looked more beautiful than ever. "Ready to face more ghosts?" she asked over her shoulder.

"Ready for everything." He caressed the wedding ring inside his lapel. And considering their recent unprotected rendezvous in the Dome Room, maybe they'd have a reason to rush "everything."

ANCIENT HISTORY

CHAPTER 11

Over the past weeks, Molly had spent some research time investigating the mysteries of Scott's past. Superior Court Judge Halston Sheridan—presumably a relative—had sealed the ancient happenings at Honey Hill, and her studies led her nowhere.

Which was why she'd swiped Scott's keys from the top of the bureau this morning before he'd awakened, and was presently en route to Port Royal, Virginia.

The drive was just over two hours, and she nearly missed the tiny town in Caroline County when she blinked. According to the welcome sign, fewer than two hundred people lived in Port Royal, which surprised her. Scott had always struck her as a metropolitan type, and he knew his way around the bigger cities in Virginia as if he'd been reared on the subway. Yet he'd hailed from a town one-tenth the size of the heritage district in Parker's Landing.

After a quick drive through the main section of the town, she opted to drive north along the Rappahannock River. The scenery rolled with tranquil laziness, a stark contrast to the hectic race to win the Monticello grant, and Molly wondered what might be so horrifying to keep a man from a paradise such as this.

Just past the Port Royal town limits, she passed a driveway on the left side of the winding road, and perhaps might not have seen it, if not for the painter touching up a sign. Because no one was behind her, she shifted into reverse and studied the cranberry-colored words on a mustard shingle. "Honey Hill."

She pulled in and rolled down the window. "Is this the Sheridan estate?"

The painter tipped his cap and nodded.

"Then I have the right place. Thank you."

"No one's here. No one's *been* here in quite some time."

"I'm Scottie's wife. And I'm here now." Leaving the hired hand staring, she followed the golden-graveled drive lined with knobby-trunk willows, as if she owned the place. Because Scott had divorced her in lieu of annulling their marriage, she could probably stake legal rights to a portion of the beautiful acreage, and she wouldn't be shy about playing that card, should the painter—or anyone else—attempt to stop her now.

Beyond an iron gate, a majestic house, in pristine condition, stood atop the hill. With the car idling, she stepped onto the stones and flipped through Scott's key ring. "All right, Gracie. Help me out with this one." The first key she selected slid into the iron gate lock as smooth as cream in cannoli, but it wouldn't turn. The second wouldn't fit, and neither did the third.

At least she knew which key *should* work, even if it wouldn't. She inserted the first key again and wiggled it until sweat dripped between her breasts. Finally, the latch popped. One lock conquered, one more to go, at the main house.

After going through the same ritual at the front door, she took a deep breath of river-scented air and entered. Having no idea why she was there, or which rooms she ought to visit, she simply wandered through empty corridors, admiring architectural details along the way.

Most of the first floor exuded happy energy. Visions of Scott during his childhood flashed in her mind, and a feeling of closeness embraced her. Why would he neglect to share this place with her? Had he never been as happy with her as he'd been here at Honey Hill?

She sat on the staircase and closed her eyes. Scents of summer flowers drifted past, as if she were traveling through time. Leather and lilacs. Piano music and after dinner mints.

To Do List: Measure this hall, floor-to-ceiling, and plan your first Christmas at Honey Hill.

A shiver raced up her spine and an impending force hovered above her. She hated this part, but she turned to face the presence, which might as well have been tugging her by the elbow up the stairs, whispering warnings along her nerve endings. *Nothing to see here. The goods are upstairs.*

When she reached the top of the stairs, she found herself trotting toward the only open door in the west wing. One step beyond the master suite threshold, the prickles on her spine spread across her back and down her arms and legs.

A gunshot.

Blood splattered against the wall, and Nathaniel Scott Sheridan, III's body slumped in a puddle of blood.

What have you done? A desperate female voice cried.

He doesn't deserve you, Ellie. I couldn't watch him lay one more hand on—

Save yourself. Give me your gun.

What are you going to do, Ellie?

Think of your career, Halston. Go!

A man's trembling hand released the firearm into her grasp, and she inadvertently squeezed the trigger.

Another discharged bullet lodged under her heart.

Oh, Ellie. My Ellie. He rocked her bleeding body. *My Ellie, I love you.*

Don't be a fool. Her eyes began to close, as she choked out her final words. *Let me go.*

Molly pinched her eyes shut and turned away in tears, but the energy of the room propelled her back. The scent of blood overpowered her, and she dropped to her knees.

Mama?

Her eyes shot open at once, although there was nothing tangible to see. She knew that voice. Scott's voice.

Mama! Not you, not you! I never would've given it to you, if I knew you'd do this! I wouldn't have, Mama, I wouldn't have! I said point it at... He turned around and faced his father's dead body. *Dad!*

Molly had seen, felt, heard, and smelled enough. And now she knew enough, too, although she wished she didn't know even a snippet of it.

Scott's parents were dead. Both of them. Ellie had a lover, who shot Nathaniel, and in turn, Ellie had accidentally shot herself. And Scott blamed himself because he'd given her a gun for protection. But the gun responsible had been—

Halston's. Halston Sheridan, the judge who had sealed the investigation records, had been responsible, had allowed an eighteen-year-old kid to carry the burden of his parents' brutal deaths.

Her cell phone buzzed at her hip, and a chilling breeze swept through the room. Although the windows and shutters were closed, the damask draperies parted, revealing a loose panel in the wainscot.

"No more." She grasped the keys in a fist and inched toward the door. "I don't want to know any more."

Her cell phone buzzed again by the time she reached the staircase, and this time, she answered it with a whimper. "Brandy! Oh, God, you'll never believe—"

"Shut up and listen. Are you there now? At the house?"

"I'm leaving. How did you know—"

"That's beside the point. It's in the wall under the window, Molly. Tell him she never used the gun. She pried off a panel and dropped it down into the wall."

"How do you know—"

"I've been having this insane dream for weeks, and I just figured out what it meant and who she was, but you have to tell him, Molly. They'll find the gun, and he can move on. With you."

"I can't talk to him about this. What I've done, what we all do with this crazy gift, Brandywine. This is none of my business, and it's none of Star's, or Dusky's, or Windy's, or yours. And I don't want to know any more."

"What makes you think we have a choice?"

Molly sank to the steps and sobbed. "I don't want it."

"He needs you, Molly. He needs you to tell him, to help him release this burden. You're wondering why you found him, when he was only destined to leave you. I'm telling you you've got it backwards. *He* found *you*, and he found you because without you, without your telling him, he'll never know true happiness. And neither will you, if you keep this from him. That blue you've been carrying around in your uterus? You're carrying it for him."

*   *   *

"Where have you been, cupcake?" From his position at the desk in their hotel room, Scott ran a hand through his rumpled hair. "I'm on pins and needles here. I don't know what to do, and you're not answering your phone."

"My phone didn't ring but once, and I'm sorry I missed your call. I was...detained."

"We lost the *tête à tête*."

Molly slumped against the door. "What? How?"

"I don't know. The donor called and said she'd changed her mind.

She's giving it to the University of Virginia, and I—"

"She's giving it to Wilkinson? But how did UVA even know we had it? Unless... Unless she saw my notes at the library."

"When?"

"A few weeks ago."

"Damn her. You should've told me she might have seen what you were working on, Mol. You should never underestimate—" He hung his head, and out of the corner of his eye, he caught sight of her, drained and wan. He stood and began in her direction. "Are you all right?"

"Scottie." She slid to the floor and hid her face in her hands. "Scottie, I'm so sorry."

"It's not your fault. We'll work around it, fake it today, and find another one when the time comes to—" He lifted her chin with a few fingers, and the fear in her eyes silenced him. She looked weak, ill even. He should have bought a pregnancy test weeks ago. "What's wrong with you?"

"I know everything about Honey Hill."

"What?"

"Everything. I know everything, and it's not what you think. It's not your—"

"How? When did you...what were—"

"I traded a Louis XV vase for information about your past, but it led me on a wild goose chase, so I took it upon myself to take a drive." She opened his palm, placed his key ring in his hand, and closed his fingers around it.

His mouth dried the instant he locked his gaze on his Honey Hill keys. He began to back away. "You mean you—"

"You have to know you weren't resp—"

"Honey Hill is my personal business, Ms. Rourke, and I don't give a damn about your ego or your acknowledgment crisis! That information was mine to share, if I ever deemed you worthy."

"I don't want to know. I wish to God I didn't!"

"And trading a period piece for information about my past? Who does that when they love someone?"

"You're one to talk! You traded me for a fake diary five years ago."

"I traded you for secrets at Honey Hill, and now I know I was right to do so, considering your lack of respect for me, my family, my—"

"Don't even think about questioning the way I feel for you. I did what I did *because* I love you. You gave me no choice."

"No choice? No choice, Miss Molly? Guess where I was going to take you—just as I've been promising to take you—after the presentation today? As difficult as it would have been for me—and make no mistake, I was not looking forward to it—I made reservations just outside Port Royal at a bed and breakfast for tonight and tomorrow night. And guess where I was going to take you next? Lexington, Virginia, to Washington and Lee University, where I spend my days and most of my nights.

"And why was I going to take you there? To see if it might be something you'd be willing to explore with me. To see if you might be willing to leave Parker's Landing behind, the way I've closed the door on Honey Hill."

"You can't close the door until you know—"

"You broke into my family's estate and stole my deepest insecurities."

"None of it was your fault, Scott. You have to know your mother never used the gun you—"

"I didn't invite you in. You have no right to know what you know."

"It was Halston. Halston shot your father."

"My mother shot my father because she couldn't take another beating. Is that what you've been dying to know all these years? Would you like me to say it again?"

"You found her, Scott."

"Yes, I did, and telling you now doesn't make the cross any easier to bear."

"You found her. Think about it, Scottie. You're missing one important detail. What did she look like?"

"I don't have time for this, and neither do you. We're due to present an incomplete project to the Thomas Jefferson Foundation in less than an hour, and we both look like hell warmed over."

"You don't have to tell me, if you'll only tell yourself. Did she look like she'd just been beaten? It wasn't self-defense. It was murder, and none of it was your—"

"Good Lord, shut up already! This grant is my right. It's there for the taking, and I'll be there presenting with or without the *tête à tête*— and with or without you."

CHAPTER 12

Scott and Molly hadn't spoken during their quick, back-to-back showers, although he had left the shower running for her, nor had they interacted during the car ride over. While he repented verbally attacking her, he felt she'd left him with little choice. He could have forgiven her for the Louis XV...hell, even for exposing her notes on the *tête à tête*, but her secret trip to Honey Hill? Her assumptions about his parents? Inexcusable.

With his ex-wife trailing a few steps behind, he entered the conference room and stopped cold when he saw Wilkinson and her team seated along the far side of the table. Molly bumped into him.

"Watch where you're going," he growled over his shoulder.

Wilkinson, with raised brows, pursed her lips. "Trouble at the Residence Inn, Dr. Sheridan?"

Molly neither apologized nor took Wilkinson's bait, but chose a seat directly across from their competition. And, damn, if his ex-wife didn't look stunning in a tailored blazer, which managed to hug each and every one of her curves.

The last thing he wanted was to make nice with her at the moment, but a united front was important. He sat next to her and looked across the table. "Did I miss a memo? Washington and Lee has the four o'clock slot, and UVA has the five-thirty, correct?"

"Apparently, you did miss something." Wilkinson rolled a pencil between her fingers. "Upon scrutiny of our preliminary concept notes, it appears we have some overlap in our presentations. Madame Curator requested both teams at once."

He was raw—too raw to go head-to-head with Wilkinson, when she'd stolen the focal point piece of his concept.

"Fake it," Molly whispered, leaning in close. "Pretend you don't know we lost it."

He pulled his glasses from where he'd tucked them at his collar and slid them onto his face. "And should I fake it when it comes to Honey Hill? Pretend you didn't do what you did?"

"Hate me for one thing at a time, if you don't mind. Better yet, hate her right now." She nodded at Wilkinson.

"Sorry I'm late." Elizabeth Varney, curator of Monticello, entered the conference room and breezed her way into the chair at the head of the table. "And Dr. Sheridan, I apologize for the surprise combined meeting, but the fax line at your hotel has been busy, and so has your cell phone."

"That's fine, Ms. Varney. Dr. Wilkinson has been good enough to fill me in."

"Time is short, so I'll cut right to the chase. We at the Thomas Jefferson Foundation find ourselves in a unique position this afternoon, ladies and gentlemen, in which we have the distinct honor of making history. We've been given two vastly different, but excellent, proposals for the dome room—one for a lover's retreat, one for a guest study suite—with the same spotlight piece, a gorgeous *tête à tête*, upholstered in a violet brocade, centered beneath the oculus. Has the piece been promised to both teams?"

Scott met Wilkinson's gaze across the table.

"I'm willing to extend some flexibility in regards to the rooms on the second floor and those remaining on the third, but I'm sure you understand, Dr. Sheridan, Dr. Wilkinson, that I cannot rely on maybes when it comes to our dome. Can anyone explain?"

Scott looked across the conference table at Wilkinson. "You stole my conversation piece?"

With gentle pressure, Molly caressed his arm. "Scottie."

For a millisecond, his wife's beauty intrigued him, but he quickly recovered from the spell and turned back to the curator. "If it's on UVA's plan, it's true. Ms. Rourke found it, I secured it, and Wilkinson stole it."

Wilkinson shot a dagger across the table. "With all due respect, Sheridan—"

"What do you know about respect?"

Elizabeth Varney cleared her throat, and instantly, the banter stopped. "Please don't tell me I have a case of I-saw-it-first on my plate. What I need to know is whether the piece is available to one or the other, or to both, or either."

Scott pulled a document from his file. "Mrs. Varney, this is correspondence from the donor, dated ten days ago, promising us the piece. We've received no written retraction."

Wilkinson produced a similar parchment. "And here's my promissory, post-marked three days ago."

"It was my idea," Scott said. "Or rather, Ms. Rourke's. So, yes, Madame Curator, I did see it first."

Wilkinson took a deep breath. "The question isn't whether your ideas precede mine, Professor Sheridan. It's a question of which team can better execute the task at hand, which is, in the event you've forgotten, the restoration of this country's most distinct home." She turned toward the curator. "Ma'am, they were banking on the *tête à tête*, and—"

"Tate-ah-tay," Molly grumbled under her breath.

"—and the simple truth is they don't have it because the owner prefers to work with the University of Virginia. It's only fitting that Jefferson's own university be given the opportunity to fulfill this task."

"Even if your team isn't as capable?" Molly asked.

"In any house of historical significance"—Wilkinson's glance hardened on Molly—"let alone Jefferson's Monticello, we must adhere to strict standards, and I won't have this house flooded with repros. The University of Virginia bows to the fact Washington and Lee outdid us on ideas perhaps, but the plain and simple truth is this: we have an academic furniture historian, who, with all due respect, Ms. Rourke, is more accustomed to working in fields of historical significance."

Scott slipped a hand into his pocket and closed his fingers around her wedding ring. "Molly's worked in some of the most historically significant homes in the Midwest, and—"

"The University of Virginia can account for every piece needed to furnish the second and third floors, as well as the attic space off the Dome, if you're so inclined to include it. Washington and Lee is close, but they fall desperately short in one crucial—"

"I have a Duncan Phyfe," Molly said. She straightened in her seat. "A sofa, an original, to replace the *tête à tête*."

Scott leaned in, whispering, "You don't have to do that."

Wilkinson waived her words. "Honey, I have an original Duncan

Phyfe sitting as a display in the President's Reception Room."

"Yes, you do," Molly tossed a curl over her shoulder. "However—"

"I don't see how your sofa proves your ability to execute," Wilkinson said. "If you had the Duncan Phyfe before, why not use it in your original plan? Are you bluffing, Ms. Rourke?" Again, she turned to the curator. "This beautifully illustrates my point, ma'am. Do you want a team willing to waiver on the plan at the last minute? Or do you want a team—"

The curator raised her hand to silence Wilkinson. "I'd like to hear more about this Duncan Phyfe, if I may."

"If a Duncan Phyfe is what you want," Wilkinson said, "the university will put ours on permanent loan."

"And I'll do the same with mine," Molly said.

"You don't have to do this for me," Scott whispered.

"I have a Duncan Phyfe and a Hepplewhite sofa table. When centered under the oculus, they'll provide a stunning focal point from any angle," offered Molly.

"The risk of shipping across country—"

"The prize far outweighs such a risk, Dr. Wilkinson. My Duncan Phyfe dates back to the early 1800s, right around the time Jefferson returned from Paris. Originally, it was housed in Philadelphia. It belonged to a diplomat who acquired the piece overseas, as he did many pieces of distinction."

"Again, ma'am, if a sofa is what you want—"

"I beg your pardon, Dr. Wilkinson," Molly said, standing and making her way around the conference table. "But your Duncan Phyfe, while prestigious in its own right, lays claim only to the backside of Elizabeth Taylor, who sat on it in the early 1980s. If you check your records, the lime green moiré taffeta used in reupholstering, while stunning in your reception room, can't hold a candle to the original Bordeaux velvet it originally boasted."

"Historically, moiré taffeta is—"

"Bear with me, Dr. Wilkinson. My Duncan Phyfe is in stunning condition, as you'll see when you check your email. As we speak, my cousin is in the process of forwarding photos to all of you." She pulled a photocopy of the piece from the file and handed it to a member of the Thomas Jefferson Foundation. "And the last backside ever to grace it belonged to Benjamin Franklin."

Scott smiled. Actually, the last piece of ass the sofa had seen had been his, but Molly was on a roll. She'd probably work wonders with the forgotten rooms at Honey Hill.

"Original upholstery?" Wilkinson asked. "Benjamin Franklin? I doubt the shelf life of velvet surpasses that of a significant historical era. How do you propose to prove it? With one of your eerie feelings?"

"I can't prove it—not to a person without extensive study of historical furniture. You'd never be able to pick it out of a line-up, for example, but your furniture expert would. Let's put it to the test. My Duncan against yours. Reupholster it in a vintage Bordeaux, and we'll let the expert from academia decide."

"I cannot reupholster it again. The Jeffries family succinctly stated—"

"Then I suggest we allow the Thomas Jefferson Foundation to make a decision without this schoolyard provocation, Dr. Wilkinson. I'm sure they're just as bored as I am with your games." Molly returned to her seat.

Scott nodded toward the members of the Thomas Jefferson Foundation. "I'm sure you have questions about other pieces. We're ready to answer them."

*   *   *

Molly exited the mansion behind Scott. The evening sun warmed her face—a much-needed comfort, considering all she'd endured that day. While she and Scott had banded together for the sake of the Monticello opportunity, nothing had changed between them since they'd left the hotel.

The past horrors of Honey Hill churned in her gut and, adding fuel to the fire, the grant was still up for grabs. At the moment, Molly hurt as much for Scott as she did because of him and his lashing out at her when she was only trying to help.

He didn't speak until Jefferson's "Little Mountain" was far behind them and then he did so with white knuckles gripping the steering wheel, as if keeping on even keel was a challenge for him. "When did you have Brandywine email pictures of your couch?"

"I haven't yet, and it's a sofa."

He nodded.

"I'm sorry about Honey Hill."

At last, he awarded her a glance, but still said nothing.

"I'll get out of your hair as soon as I pack my things," she said.

"You don't have to do that. I just need time."

"How do you feel about the grant?"

"What my gut says?" He licked his lips. "It's not mine."

"Then I suppose there's no reason for me to stay. You sought me to help you win this project, and what's done is done."

"We gave it our best shot, I suppose."

"Manifest Destiny, right? But what happens when you claim something you're not sure you want?"

He shot her a quick, emerald stare, but only shook his head.

Her eyes welled with tears. "It wasn't easy feeling what I felt at Honey Hill, you know. You're hurting, you've been hurting, and it kills me to know you'd rather push me away than let me help you."

"Maybe we both need time."

"You gave your mother a gun. For protection."

"I don't have to rely on your odd ability to know what happened there, Molly. I know because I lived it, and I don't want to live it again."

"But you're living it every day. You'll continue to live it until you know the whole truth. She never used the gun. She—"

"Enough!"

"She pried off a panel beneath the west window—"

"I don't want to—"

"But you have to hear it, whether you want to or not." She wiped a tear from her cheek. "You don't want me anymore? I can live with that. I've lived with it for five years, and as impossible as it seems, I'll find a way to do it again. But I can't live knowing what I know, when you don't know the whole truth."

"The truth is sealed in a court file, and it's sealed up here." He tapped his temple with a finger.

"She dropped the gun down into the wall. It was Halston who killed your father."

"It was Halston who secured the gun for me. You've got things wrong."

"Find Halston. Ask him to explain what was going on between him and your mother."

"Halston's dead. He died last year."

"Then you have to open the wall."

"This is crazy. You're wrong."

"Ellie accidentally shot herself—in the heart, not the head. Right?"

"Yeah." He nodded. "In the heart."

"Most suicidal shooters blow their brains out, Scottie, to end it quickly, so they won't feel it. I'm going back to Parker's Landing, but you should go back to Honey Hill. If I'm wrong, if there's not a gun in that wall, feel free to believe what you've always believed."

"And you're just going to go? Just like that?"

"I can't wait for *America Windows*, or what they represent, and looking at you now, you don't want me to."

* * *

At six in the morning, Scott meandered onto the terrace, searching for serenity, but the fog in the mountains prohibited much of any view. It was only fitting; today he would lose her, and, in effect, lose everything. Those neglecting to study history are only doomed to repeat it, he'd often told his students. He was fast becoming evidence that proved the theory.

A bright yellow taxi appeared in the parking lot below, and a colorful woman, carrying only a tote bag, stepped out. She looked up, as if she knew he'd been there, watching her approach.

"Hey, stranger." She tickled the air with a few fingers. "How's my cousin?"

One word came to him, and while it wasn't a word he often used to describe a person, it dripped off his tongue like dew off a leaf. "Blue."

Brandywine shrugged. "So how do you want to do this? You wanna come down? Should I come up? Or should we wake the entire establishment with our current arrangement?"

"I'll come down. She needs the sleep."

His unexpected visitor raised an eyebrow. "Don't be all day about it, and don't bother looking in the mirror. I assure you, you look every bit as hellish as you feel."

A few moments later, she embraced him on the sidewalk.

"Did Molly know you're coming?"

Merlot curls bounced against her shoulders when she shook her head. "No, but Star and I thought I should be here. Either to help her pack, or to hold her while you walk away."

"Who says I'm walking anywhere?"

Again, her eyebrow peaked. "You don't know much about the women in our family, do you? Come on. I'm famished. Let's hit breakfast."

They turned toward the hotel restaurant. "Listen, about what she did at Honey Hill."

He stiffened. "Does the whole world know?"

"Oh, for crying out loud. You're uncomfortable with me knowing?

134

Try waking up to the scene night after night after night."

"I do."

"All right, then you know where I'm coming from." She entered the restaurant and sank onto a bench with a green-and-white striped cushion. "She was drawn to your childhood home, and she followed the pull because she didn't have a choice. Understand it, accept it, and make a choice of your own. Do you want to live the rest of your life as a victim? Or do you want to live, period?"

"Two?" A hostess appeared with menus.

"Two." Brandywine grinned. "And good morning." They followed to a remote table and sat. "It's like Molly and this issue with food. She has a crazy ideal in her head, and she's constantly battering herself to stick to it. You're doing the same thing with your family."

He turned over his mug. He'd need a lot of caffeine, if he was going to keep up with Molly's cousin.

"You have this beautiful estate," she continued. "This gorgeous shell is sitting high atop a hill, a geographic pedestal, if you will. On the inside, that shell's deteriorated, but you think if you look at it from a distance, if you keep it boarded up and safe from the weather, you can keep it as ideal as it is in your mind. Am I right?"

"I'm listening."

"The point is this. No matter how pretty it is, those walls know the ugly things that happened there. You don't have to like it, but the sooner you acknowledge it, the better off you'll be. Just as Molly will be a hell of a lot healthier once she releases the one-hundred-ten syndrome."

"One-hundred-ten what?"

"It's the weight she never surpasses."

"She's at one-twenty-two."

Brandywine's lips parted, and her face took on an awestruck expression. She rose from her chair, walked around the table and pressed her hands against his cheeks. "One-twenty-two?"

He nodded. "She wasn't happy about it, but she looks gr—"

She threw her arms around him and squeezed. "Thank you."

"Coffee?" A waitress appeared with two pots.

Scott nodded. "Regular for me." He pointed to Brandywine's mug. "But if you give her any more energy, she'll explode."

*   *   *

"Molly."

135

A finger brushed against her cheek and then trailed along her bottom lip.

"Wake up, cupcake."

She opened her eyes and looked into Scott's. *To Do List: Write a dissertation on the mesmerizing stare of Scott Sheridan.* "Hi."

"I didn't want to go without saying goodbye." He pulled her into his arms and raked into her hair. "Brandywine's here. She arrived this morning."

"Brandy?"

"She'll make the trip back with you."

Molly looked at the clock. Nearly nine? "I'm sorry I overslept. I don't know why I'm so tired lately. I—"

"I bought a pregnancy test. If you don't want to take it before you go, that's fine, but you should take it soon."

"I'm not pregnant."

"Either way, let me know. I have to straighten out a few things here, but—"

"Then straighten things out. Don't worry about my uterus."

"Part of me hopes you give me a reason."

"Don't say that. You don't mean it."

"I always say what I mean. You should know that by now." He tightened his embrace. "Let me know."

She pinched her eyes shut, and Chagall's *America Windows* materialized in her mind. She rubbed a thumb over the scar on his shoulder. "Goodbye."

CHAPTER 13

Scott lingered on the upstairs landing at Honey Hill, with his cell phone ringing in his pocket. Wilkinson was calling. He hadn't rented a car, driven two hours in the opposite direction of Washington and Lee, and allowed Molly to head back to Chicago so he could listen to Wilkinson gloat over the grant. He had personal business to close, and if he didn't close it, he'd have come all this way for nothing.

He kneaded a piece of gum between his molars and walked to the master suite. The heavy air smelled like the lilacs Ellie Sue had often kept on her dressing table. He sniffed again, but the aroma had faded, leaving him to believe he had imagined it. A familiar creepy, crawly sensation tickled up his spine.

Of all the places in this world, he did not want to be here. Odd that he couldn't bear facing the demons in the house, yet wouldn't consider selling it. He neared the window and parted the drapes. Nothing seemed out-of-ordinary. He sank to the floor upon which his parents had perished, and leaned against the wainscot.

The wall creaked behind him, and suddenly, the horrific, fifteen-year-old scene replayed in his mind. He dropped his head into his hands, willing the image to disappear, but it persisted and zeroed in on Ellie Sue's beautiful, lifeless body lying in a pool of blood.

Scott couldn't gain control of his rapid breathing, and sweat broke out on his back and on his neck. The walls seemed to be closing in on him. He scrambled toward the door, but couldn't find his footing. With tears blurring his vision, he inched toward the sanctuary of the hallway, where he regained his composure and looked again. No bodies, no blood.

He exhaled slowly, face to face with the ghosts of his past, at last. He'd never forget the sight of her. Pale in death, yet still lovely. At peace. And...and without a bruise on her body. Molly was right.

With tentative steps, he entered the room and approached the window once more, this time pressing his hands against the panel. It felt sturdy and secure, yet the center bowed. He pushed against the center again and felt it knock against the plaster.

He'd need a crowbar to remove it. On a mission now, he ventured out to the stable to retrieve a pry bar. He kicked up dirt and whatever was left of his father's ashes as he passed the pony stall. "Hi, Dad."

He retrieved the tool and hurried back to the master suite. With one forceful shove, he buried the lip of the bar between the window sill and the panel and began to pry. After a few minutes of persistence, the wood budged. He jerked it from the wall to reveal a jagged hole in the plaster, just big enough for him to reach inside.

With a steady hand, he maneuvered in and snaked around, but he felt nothing but cobwebs and house. More plaster broke away, and he reached further toward the floor.

His fingers met a thin, cylindrical item, not unlike the barrel of a gun. He pulled his arm free and hacked at the wall with the crowbar until chunks of plaster fell free to reveal the gun he'd purchased as an eighteen-year-old kid, along with a single envelope of his mother's lilac-scented stationery.

Centered on the front, in black ink, his mother had scrawled in feminine script "Scott."

CHAPTER 14

"Thursday toast." Star raised a shot of wheatgrass in salute. "To the extra meat on Molly's bones. May she learn to love it."

"Here, here." Brandywine threw back the shot.

With a grimace after a tasting, Molly tossed the contents of her glass into the farm sink. She'd been back for two weeks, and it was business as usual in Parker's Landing. Disgusting concoctions, dance class, no word from her husband...

Star crooked a finger. "Come here."

...and clairvoyant relatives. "I'm fine, Star."

"You're blue."

Molly approached her aunt with slow steps. "Yeah, I'm blue. I'm going to be blue until I deal with losing him again, but I'm all right. I'll make it. I have all of you."

The kitchen light gleamed off Star's signature gold ring when she patted Molly's abdomen. "Hmm."

"All right." Molly threw her hands into the air. "I know I'm chubby—"

"Healthy," Brandywine corrected.

"But I'm not pregnant. Would you two be convinced if I took the test right now?"

"Pee fast, or we'll be late for dance," Brandywine said.

Molly's cell phone buzzed at her hip, and after a glance at the caller ID screen, she caught sight of a familiar area code. "It's him!" Her heart pounded with joy, and she brought the phone to her ear. "Hi!"

"Ms. Rourke?" Not Scott. Not even a man.

She pulled the phone from her ear and again checked the number, and found she didn't recognize it.

"Ms. Rourke, this is Elizabeth Varney, curator of Monticello."

"Oh, yes. Hello, Ms. Varney."

"Dr. Wilkinson and the University of Virginia have offered the *tête à tête* for use in the lover's retreat, in exchange for mention in the donator's record, but I'm intrigued with the story about your Duncan Phyfe."

"I beg your pardon?"

"The Duncan Phyfe. Benjamin Franklin."

"Yes, I know the sofa, but I'm a little confused about the grant."

"Hasn't Dr. Sheridan contacted you? We've awarded it to Washington and Lee."

"Sorry, I hadn't heard."

"I suppose he's been busy since we offered him the project, but I'm curious. Suppose we use the *tête à tête* in the Dome Room, as well as the Duncan Phyfe? Would you still be willing to donate it?"

Molly lowered her numb body to the breakfast table. He'd won. And he hadn't called to inform her.

"Ms. Rourke?"

Molly shook her head. "Of course you can have it." *Anything for Thomas Jefferson.* "I'll make arrangements for its delivery."

"Oh, that won't be necessary. I'll send a truck. We'll be in touch in the next few weeks, and, Ms. Rourke, I cannot tell you how pleased we at the Thomas Jefferson Foundation are to have involved you in this endeavor. Your input will help to restore this country's finest historical residence to a pinnacle thus far unseen."

"Thank you for the opportunity." At least someone was pleased enough with her work to acknowledge it. "Goodbye, Ms. Varney, and thanks for the call." She snapped her phone closed and blinked away tears. She'd donate the sofa, but no more of her time. She and Monticello—like she and her husband—had parted ways, no matter how amazing their experience could have been.

"Girlfriend, what's—"

"He won." Molly stood and hiked her dance bag over her shoulder. "He won the opportunity of a lifetime, and he hasn't called to share it with me."

"More like you won it for him, and he's claiming the prize." Brandywine hooked an arm around Molly's waist. "You deserve so much more. I'm gonna kick his ass, I swear."

"I suppose I know where I stand now. Thomas Jefferson." She held her hand as high as she could reach. "Me." She lowered her hand to waist level and turned in the direction opposite the front door.

"Where are you going?" her cousin asked.

"I'm going to take the test, to be rid of him once and for all." She charged into the powder room, ripped open the test she'd carried with her since she'd left Virginia, and wiggled out of her sleeveless, one-piece leotard.

Once she'd saturated the stick, she set it on the vanity and joined her family in the kitchen. "All right, you can check it in a few minutes. I'm going to class."

"You can't just go without looking at it!"

"Brandy, believe me. It's negative."

"What are you going to do if you're pregnant?" Brandywine asked.

"Nothing. I'm not, and if the two of you need to see a negative result that badly, go have a look."

Brandywine darted back to the powder room.

"Besides, I've already lost three pounds." Molly wiped a tear from her eye. "Nine more to go. Minimum."

"I know why you're doing this," Star said. "You can control your weight, but you can't control him. Don't sacrifice your health simply because you can."

"That's not what I'm doing." She tunneled through the hallway under the stairs and stepped over the sheepdog perpetually filling the foyer floor. Molly reached for Buddha's belly. "Good karma, Chubs. Good karma."

The bells of Saint Andrews tolled the hour of six as she exited the house. Brandywine fell in stride beside her as she crossed Park Avenue and continued along Whitney Street.

"Tell me about this new guy." Molly wiped away a budding tear.

"Now's hardly the time, Mol."

"If not now, if not on the drive from Charlottesville, if not anytime over the past two weeks, when? I may as well be happy for someone, and you deserve it. So tell me."

Brandywine made the mistake of hesitating.

"Tell me, damn it! What's he like?"

"Okay, okay. First of all, he's not new. I've been seeing him for six months."

"Six months? And no one's met him yet?"

"Hey, you married someone before bringing him home to meet the fam, so don't start."

"I guess so." She chewed her lip. "Call it even?"

"Yeah." Brandywine laid her head against Molly's shoulder. "You're my sister."

"You're my sister, too."

"I'd sell my soul if he'd come back for you."

"I'm fine, Brandy."

"You're not fine. You're crying."

"Damn, I'm going to miss that Duncan Phyfe." She stomped her foot, spun into Brandywine's arms, and cried on her cousin's shoulder. Fresh memories of making love with Scott—who was she kidding, of loving him, period—burned in her heart. Losing him was a fresh wound, too deep for a bandage. She needed professional help in stitching this one.

"We don't have to go to dance class, if you don't want to." Brandywine smoothed Molly's bun. "You want to over-indulge a little? Eat a cookie, or even a cake, at Susie's Sweets? Chocolate-covered strawberries? I know how you love fruit."

Molly stifled a laugh.

"I have something to show you." Brandywine extended a snack-size Zip-lock bag.

"What is it?"

"It's a positive pregnancy test."

Molly took the bag. "Positive?" The words sounded foreign, displaced, but the proof was right there. "But I was so sure... I know my body, and I was—"

"It isn't your test, Molly." Brandywine took it back, and a faint smile touched her lips. "It's mine."

Molly might have been concerned, if not for the apparent elation spreading across her cousin's face. "Brandy..."

"Seems Star isn't the only one to come into her sixth sense when she was about to become a mother."

"Does she know?"

"No, but she'll know soon enough. Baby energy. She'll know it's coming from somewhere."

Molly hugged her cousin. "This is big news!"

"I'm gestating the next generation of freakish women who see well beyond what the rest of the world sees." Brandywine smiled. "And I love him."

"That's good."

"I only wish Scott knew what he had in you."

*   *   *

In the confines of Amelia's Dance Connection, Molly propped her leg on the highest *barre* and pressed her chest to her knee. It felt good to stretch again, good to work her muscles in a way that didn't involve screaming her ex-husband's name.

She looked again to the door. Why did she expect him to appear? The sooner she warmed up to the idea of never seeing him again, the better. She didn't need him anyway. She'd been just fine for five whole years without him, and she'd survive the next fifty, if she had to.

But wouldn't it have been grand to spend the next fifty years with the man she'd married? She imagined children laughing and playing at Honey Hill, piano music filling the front parlors, while they decorated a Christmas tree in the center hall. Summer walks through lilac-filled gardens. Yearly consummations at Monticello's Honeymoon Gazebo, in the Dome Room at sundown. They'd even do it on the grounds of Tuckahoe plantation—once and for all.

"Molly?"

"Huh?" She blinked into her cousin's gaze, as her classmates filed past on their way out the door.

"Time to go."

"Oh." Molly pulled her leg from the *barre*. In a daze she followed the others into the lobby, where she changed shoes.

"Did you eat today?" Brandywine asked.

"Don't start. I can't do this today. I can't."

The girls walked westward down Center Street and continued along Whitney. "You're acting flaky. You act flaky when you don't eat."

"I'm fine. Flaky because the past couple of months have been insane, but fine." She vowed not to look up, toward her house, for fear she may imagine him sitting on her front porch steps, and instead walked quickly along the cobblestone, with her head down.

"Call me later." At the intersection of Whitney and Park, Brandywine tugged Molly's sleeve and turned toward Westerfield Place. "Or better yet, I'll call you."

"Sure." Molly looked toward her home. No history professor waited there today. *Or ever would.* Perhaps if she convinced herself it all had been a dream...

She meandered across Park Avenue and up her brick drive. The porch steps proved a difficult to climb today, as, for a fleeting moment, she could have sworn she felt him there, awaiting her.

A ringing telephone beyond the threshold propelled her into her home, and tingles of passion settled in her skin. The memory of his awaiting her at this place would now haunt her forever. There was no escaping him now, not that there ever was.

Floor boards creaked above her. "Give it a rest, Gracie, will you?" *To Do List: Teach the resident ghost to dance; she'll be lighter on her feet.*

She raced into the kitchen and answered the phone.

"Molly, it's Star. You must find the hatbox."

"Hatbox? I thought for sure you'd be calling with my test results."

"Do you want to know?"

"No, I already know. I know my body down to my metabolic rate." *And the baby energy you're feeling is coming from your daughter.*

"Are you sure about that?"

Molly sighed. "What about the hatbox?"

"You know the one I'm talking about. In it are the answers you've been seeking. Does he love you? Does he need you? Will he forsake all others for you?"

"There's nothing in that hatbox but old, worn-out mementos, and I haven't seen it in months. I have piles of laundry to do, two bathrooms to clean, and an ex-husband to forget. I can't look for anything tonight, and even if I could, I don't have the energy to rifle through it."

"You can't afford not to. It's urgent."

This wasn't anyone's business but hers. Why couldn't her family leave her to wallow in peace? While they meant well, she often wished none of them—especially she, herself—had the gift of second sight, but never so much as she did now. Without her eerie capability, Scott never would have left her for fear she'd discover his family secrets, and they'd most likely be together now, celebrating their fifth wedding anniversary.

"Molly?"

"I'll try to find the time."

"The only thing you're allowed to do before you look for it is eat. Want me to send over a plate?"

"No, I have leftover Chinese."

"Goodnight." Star hung up the phone.

Stories above her, a door closed with a click. It seemed even Gracie wouldn't relent until Molly faced the demons in some cranny of the attic. "All right, you win. I'm coming."

She walked back through every furniture-filled room toward the staircase. After spending days on end at Monticello, this house seemed awfully small and cramped. She dragged a hand over the arm of her Duncan Phyfe sofa in a loving caress. Her parlor would soon be minus one distinct piece, which she'd sacrificed for Scott.

To be fair, she'd surrendered it for the sake of the Monticello grant. Could it be she shared her ex-husband's passion for restoration? Did she, too, desire to see Jefferson's lady become the best she could be, regardless of cost or casualty?

Whatever. While Monticello shone with glory, Molly would soon be without her prized sofa—and without her man—and that was the size of it.

She pattered up the first flight of stairs, rounded the corner and took on the steps to the attic, where a light burned, pouring a stream out from her private dance studio. Thus far, no electrician had been able to find an explanation for the random flickering on and off of the lights on the third floor. *To Do List: Call for another opinion, just to make sure there isn't a short.* "I don't own stock in the electric company, Gracie."

"On behalf of your poltergeist roommate—" Scott stepped out from behind the studio door, and Molly jumped.

He smiled. "I apologize."

"Jeez, Scottie!" She placed a hand over her thumping heart and worked to catch her breath. A smile escaped her, but she quickly concealed it. She straightened to a ramrod third position and raised an eyebrow.

With a smile peaking at one corner of his mouth, he tapped the Sally Hemings paperback into his palm. "Have you heard? We won."

She took a step closer, and even as she savored the male scent of him, she pummeled her fists into his chest. "Why do you assume you can turn up here, smile, and—"

"Good to see you, too, cupcake."

"Don't lay that drawl on me."

"I'm not laying anything on you." He pulled her close and brushed his cheek against hers. "Yet."

His lips nuzzling her ear were heaven. "And that's *my* book. You bought it for me, remember?"

He dropped the book to the floor and pulled her close. "Again, my apologies."

He smelled of cinnamon gum and probably tasted of it, too.

Involuntarily, her eyes closed, and she arched into him, enjoying the feel of his mouth at her neck.

"I've missed you." His whisper misted over her every private part, and his fingers trailed up her spine, priming her.

She cherished the feeling of him, as if he were a lackadaisical summer breeze—refreshing, carefree. Inch by masculine inch, he surrounded her, secured her as he pressed his mouth to her shoulder. "Where the hell have you been?"

"Honey Hill, Monticello, *America Windows*."

"What were you doing at the Art Institute?"

"Facing demons."

"Ohhh. Interesting."

"I'll show you interesting."

She knew his brand of "interesting," and after indulging in it for weeks on end, she'd been craving him like ice cream. "Please." She peeled her eyes open, ready to yank the shirt from his torso. But out of the corner of her eye, she saw the very object she'd been on her way to retrieve. The mysterious hatbox sat—with contents spilling out—not twelve inches from where their make-out session was starting.

"Where'd you find that?" She nodded toward the open treasure trove.

He glanced and continued making love to her neck with his mouth. "Right where it is."

"But I looked. You looked." She dropped to her knees and reached for the box. "We looked."

He sighed and crouched at her side. "Diabolical, isn't it?"

"And it was here? Just…sitting here?"

"You kept every little thing, didn't you?" He grasped the shirt she'd stashed away. "Wine corks, plantation entry tickets, that god-awful poem I wrote for you. Our divorce papers. And you know, I looked for this shirt for weeks."

"You can't have it." She snatched it away. "It's part of my divorce settlement. And I love that sonnet, thank you very much."

He let out a chuckle. "Lord, that was terrible. There's a reason I'm not published in poetry journals."

She fished the poem from the box and meandered toward her ballet *barre*. With a leg propped, she read:

And forever blue,
Little Mountain top;

I beg of red to warm her;
without it all,
his heart will stop;
sleepless in a corner.

Little mountain. An overt reference to Monticello, yet she'd never caught it before. Red alluded to her hair, maybe, and "sleepless," to his familial discontent. Star was correct, from a certain point of view, when she predicted Molly would find salvation in the hatbox. The lines scrawled on that paper answered her insecurities, and the sonnet had been sleeping in the hatbox for half a decade.

But now it was time for a field test. Could the author stand behind his words? "Scottie, it really is—"

"You look incredible, you know that?" He approached her with steady steps. "When you smile, when you sleep." He licked his lips. "When you eat, when you dream."

"I'm a mess."

"I like you this way." He pulled a pin from her bun. "One." He twirled the hairpin and bent to kiss her.

"What's changed?" Before his lips met hers, she slipped away. "What's changed between us?"

"Plenty."

"I haven't heard from you in weeks."

"You're hearing from me now." With a liquid motion, he lowered himself to the floor and pulled her atop him. She found herself straddling him, looking down at his cocky smile.

"What makes you think you can stroll in here, unannounced—not once, but twice now—and steal my hairpins? I am not an object, intended to fulfill your Manifest Destiny complex."

"No, you're not." He sat up, creating a lap for her and again closing the gap between them, and tucked a flyaway ringlet behind her ear. "But that doesn't make you any less mine."

Her cheeks flushed with the fire he stoked within her. "What makes you think…" No matter how hard she tried, she couldn't raise her voice above a whisper.

"I've seen that look in your eyes before, Miss Molly." His lips met hers in a gentle caress. "Now, if you'll be good enough to tell me, how many pins am I looking for today?"

"Twenty." She breathed the number more than spoke it.

"One." He twirled the pin he'd already pulled and dropped it to the floor. "Two." He yanked another.

She raised her chin and closed her eyes, in anticipation of his kiss.

He trailed the pin along her lower lip. "My mother had a vivacious spirit."

She opened her eyes and felt her brow furrow amid her confusion. *No kiss?*

"Three." He pulled another. "She married a man with a temper. Four. Although I didn't know it until recently, she found solace in the arms of my uncle."

"Scottie, you don't have to tell me—"

"Yes, I do. Five. When my father discovered her secret, his rage overtook him. And thus, the beatings began."

She cradled his face in her hands. "I'm sorry."

"Six. Over the course of many years, I stepped in only once. It resulted in a lash across my back, courtesy of the whip he used to discipline the horses."

Her hands trailed to the scar on his right shoulder blade, and she nudged in closer, with her hair becoming heavier as fewer pins secured it.

"Seven. The cut on my shoulder healed, but in fifteen years, I haven't forgotten the bite of that whip. Eight. I commissioned the help of Halston in protecting my mother. Nine. It appears he'd already planned to protect her—with a gun of his own."

She wove her hands into his hair. He pulled free another hairpin.

"Ten. Ellie didn't trust my father with a gun in the house, so she hid it, where she had access to it, should she need it, but somewhere his large hands couldn't reach. Eleven. I'll never know if Halston intended to scare my father, or if he intended to kill him. Twelve."

With the removal of the twelfth pin, her hair fell into her face, and he swept it aside.

"Twelve is a big one. Along with the gun, my mother dropped a letter behind the panel, posthumously explaining her dilemma, things she never voiced during her lifetime. She didn't leave a reason for the letter, or mention why she hid it, or how she expected I'd find it. Something divine in that, I'm sure."

"I think so."

"And now the weight is off my shoulders. I don't mess with guilt." He gave a small shrug. "Not guilt about my mother anyway." His hands wandered through her curls and pulled pins as he found them. As he called them out, he dropped them to the floor. "Thirteen, fourteen, fifteen. I met an amazing woman," he said against her lips. "I married her, and I lost her."

"You never lost me." She parted her lips and invited his tongue to play.

He held her firmly against his hard body, with one hand between her shoulder blades and the other massaging her head and dislodging hairpins as they kissed.

"Sixteen," she murmured.

"Washington and Lee won the grant."

"I know that already. Try again."

"Wilkinson forfeited that weird chair to the Jefferson Foundation. "

She ground her pelvis against the stiffening member in his jeans. "Congratulations."

He kissed a thank you onto her mouth, "For everything," dropped a few more hairpins to the floor, and peeled the unitard over her shoulders. "Seventeen, eighteen, nineteen."

She inched his Washington and Lee t-shirt up and pulled at his belt.

"We'll never make it to twenty, if you go there." He nipped her lips.

"I'll take my chances."

"My sisters can't wait to meet you." He opened her bra clasp and returned to continue his search for the remaining hairpin. "Renee's thirty-eight; she's pregnant. Hannah's thirty-five; also pregnant. How about you? Are you pregnant, too?"

"No." Molly released his cock from its denim prison. She kneaded his shaft from one end to the other. "But two out of three ain't bad."

He drew in a long breath and shoved her clothing further down her ribcage. She raised her hips, enabling him to move the garment over her rear. He lifted her legs to his shoulder and yanked the dancewear clean off her body.

The final pin fell from her hair.

As she stroked him, his eyes closed and he breathed, "Molly."

"Thanks for coming."

"I didn't have a choice." He retracted, slipping through her hands.

"What do you mean, you—"

By the time she rose to a seated position, he knelt in front of her, erection peeking out of his fly. "Some things are determined long before we realize there's a decision to be made. What do you say, Molly? Let's let the gods of fate decide this one for us." He revealed a deck of cards. "Heart, we get married."

Although she shook her head, she couldn't help smiling. "History's repeating itself."

He fanned the cards and shrugged. "Well, that's up to you."

She selected one and turned it over. "Jack of Spades. Better luck next time. And speaking of getting lucky…" She hooked a finger through a belt loop and yanked on his jeans.

He dropped the deck into his pocket. When he withdrew his hand, it was with a white gold and sapphire ring in his grasp. "Then what do you say we do this the right way?"

"What?"

"I've looked into a few options. Northwestern University. Big Ten School, and it's just a Metra ride away from Parker's Landing. I may be able to catch a faculty seat there in the fall, and hey, I can fish all summer long in Gray's Lake."

"But you won."

"And if Northwestern doesn't pan out, I can teach junior college for a while, wait for something to open up."

"You can't do that. You're too good. I can't keep you from Virginia. You just won the damned opportunity of a lifetime, Scottie! I can't—"

"Well, there's always door number three. Summers and vacations here, semesters in Lexington." He chewed his lip for a moment, and his eyes seemed a brighter shade of emerald. "I know you're close to your family. I know this is a lot to ask."

"Yes," she whispered.

"But I think you'll like my family, too, once you get to know them. Molly Catherine Rourke—"

"Yes." She blinked from the ring to his gaze and again yanked on his jeans, this time more forcefully. "Yes!"

*   *   *

He caught himself before he crashed against her lovely, nude body and backed off to study her. Her hair—with its scent of lilac—spilled against the natural maple floor like an auburn bouquet of wild flowers framing her face. "Marry me again."

"Yes," she whispered, when he slid the ring onto her finger. She laced her hands into his hair.

As he worked his way between her legs, she hooked a toe into his waistband and pushed his jeans off with her feet. Next, she gathered his t-shirt into small folds in her hands and worked it over his head.

He grasped her supple thigh and massaged a smooth leg. She hadn't noticed yet, but he'd found his wedding ring in the hatbox and put it on while she read that hokey poem. No need to call it to her attention. She'd feel the band of white gold soon enough.

"Baby, I—"

"I love you, too." He slipped his left ring finger to her moist folds and slowly screwed it into her opening. Her juices seeped beneath his ring when he rubbed it more blatantly against her, spurring memories of the sweet twenty-three days she'd been his wife, conjuring images of the days yet to come.

He curled his finger against her walls, catching the tender spots inside her.

She bit her lip and her brow began to knit as she gave in to the pleasure. Her hips bucked upward, meeting his thrusting digit. Before long, she brought her own hand down and rubbed circles on her clit. "I want it," she whispered.

Lord, he knew she did. He entered her with two fingers at once, stretching her, filling her, and lowered his head between her thighs. The feminine scent of her, post-ballet workout, sent a surge of joy straight up his cock.

He flattened his tongue at the south side of her slit and licked the perimeter to her nub, tasting a sweet palette of woman, closing his lips around her fingers and the hyper-sensitive button they entertained. His free hand traveled over her flat abdomen to fondle a breast. She squeezed his hand, the flickering light bulb above reflecting off her ring.

Her breathing became erratic and heavy, and the sight of the antique jewelry on her hand aroused him even further.

"So right." Her strained words voiced his exact thoughts.

He blew onto her and plunged three fingers into her vagina; she moved her fingers faster.

His balls tightened with the need for release, but it was too soon, and this—working together to make things as right as they possibly could be—was a good start. He stroked her internally with precision and lapped at her clit like a thirsty dog, sucking, rubbing, licking her fingers.

"Scott."

Cum spiraled in his testes, so ready, and he hummed against her with the pre-orgasmic feeling.

She tightened her grip on his hand at her breast. "Scott." Her fingers moved at warp speed down below, as if she could start a fire with skin-on-skin friction.

He dragged his tongue along her inner thigh as he backed away. He aligned his shaft with her channel and dove in.

The lights flickered off and on again.

A hot geyser erupted around his prick, and her fingers stilled at her favorite spot. She was coming. Hard. So hard that sweat covered her body like a fine rain, and she cried out in pleasure.

"Scott!"

He grasped her hands and pinned them over her head, as he pushed into her, urging her to continue. "Don't stop."

She dragged a finger over his wedding band and a breath caught in her throat. "Oh, Scottie." Her tension slowly subsided, but her cheeks remained flushed and he felt her rushing pulse deep inside her.

With one last plunge, and unable to further delay his climax, he spilled into her.

She locked her legs around his waist.

Their mouths met in a gentle caress, and she sighed in satisfaction.

"Who knew the missionary position could be that much fun?" He nuzzled her beautiful neck, while she laughed.

Footsteps sounded on the steps.

"Go away, Gracie," he said. "We're busy."

CHAPTER 15

"Molly!"

The footsteps grew louder and closer. Scott reached for the hatbox and pulled his old shirt from it, while, beneath him, Molly struggled to grasp more discarded clothing. But he was still inside her, and semen seeped out with their movement. *To Do List: Start a regimen of birth control. Or*—she smiled—*conceive.*

"Molly, where are you?"

Scott spread the shirt over his bare ass just in time and covered her body with his.

Half a second after Brandywine peeked in, she ducked back out of the studio. "Oh my, Amin Ra, haven't you two ever heard of a bed?"

"Beg your pardon, ma'am." Scott withdrew and tossed Molly the shirt he'd used to cover himself. "But haven't you ever heard of a doorbell?"

"Something tells me you wouldn't have answered anyway, but until recently, this has never been a problem."

"I'll take that as a compliment." Scott shoved his legs into his blue jeans and sealed his mouth around Molly's in a deep kiss.

"I'll come back in a few," Brandywine said. "Days, maybe?"

"You can come in now." Molly patted Scott's nude chest and admired the ring on her finger.

"Are you sure?" Brandywine peeked before entering. "I told Star about the baby."

"How'd it go?" Molly adjusted the button on her shirt.

153

"She's obsessed with the blue in your uterus."

"For once, I assure you. I'm not blue."

"That's not what Star says." Brandywine tossed a small, rectangular box to Scott.

As he opened the package, Molly peered over his shoulder and yelped with joy at the object inside.

"The blue in your uterus is a boy," Brandywine said with a grin. "Conceived later than you suspected, when your body was ready for it, in a place of historical significance."

"I believe that would be the Dome Room at Jefferson's Monticello." Scott looked up from the positive pregnancy test and pressed a hand against Molly's abdomen. His green eyes shone with the intensity of a lifetime of love, partnership, and responsibility ahead of them.

"Lover's retreat, indeed." Molly parted her lips, ready to accept her husband's kiss.

"I'll leave you to celebrate." Brandywine pattered down the stairs. "And don't forget to eat! Star's orders!"

Scott brushed Molly's chin with his thumb. "Hungry?"

"Starving."

The lights flickered off the moment their mouths met. "Thanks, Gracie," they said in unison.

PENNY DAWN

All right, so who among us doesn't have a few demons to exorcise?

Penny Dawn began her writing career at the tender age of seven, before she realized it's impossible to be All Good, All the Time…at least in the religious sense (grinning like a Cheshire.) Romantic stories with passionate twists have since become this Good Girl's forte…and she unleashes her demons on paper, over and over and over again.

Penny Dawn holds a B. A. in history and English from Northern Illinois University and an M. A. in Creative Writing from Seton Hill University, whose alumnae include spicy novelists Jacki King, Shannon Hollis, Suzanne Forster, Dana Marton, and others. When she isn't writing, Penny enjoys tap, ballet, and jazz dance, photography, physical fitness, and renovating her 1906 Victorian Lady with her husband and two daughters.

Drop by her web site www.pennydawn.com to discuss all things decadent

AMBER QUILL PRESS, LLC
THE GOLD STANDARD IN PUBLISHING

QUALITY BOOKS
IN BOTH PRINT AND ELECTRONIC FORMATS

ACTION/ADVENTURE

SCIENCE FICTION

MAINSTREAM

FANTASY

ROMANCE

HISTORICAL

YOUNG ADULT

SUSPENSE/THRILLER

PARANORMAL

MYSTERY

EROTICA

HORROR

WESTERN

NON-FICTION

AMBER QUILL PRESS, LLC
http://www.amberquill.com

2125898

Made in the USA